Carol M.Creasey

UNITED WRITERS
Cornwall

UNITED WRITERS PUBLICATIONS LTD
Ailsa, Castle Gate, Penzance, Cornwall.
www.unitedwriters.co.uk

British Library Cataloguing in Publication Data:
A catalogue record for this book is
available from the British Library.

ISBN 9781852002152

*All characters and events in this publication
are completely fictitious.*

Printed and bound in Great Britain by
United Writers Publications Ltd.,
Cornwall.

In loving memory of
my dear brother Ronnie,
always in our thoughts.

Chapter One

"Leave me alone. You have no idea what I am going through!" said Chloe Ward, her face red and her eyes full of tears. "I need to get out of here!"

Stephen, her husband, tried to calm her by speaking gently. "Come back in, sweetheart, and let's talk about it." But his words had no effect on her. She ran quickly down the steps of their Victorian house, and set off by foot along Stone Road.

Brian Jefferies, who lived next door, was out in his front garden doing some weeding on this warm day in May, so he could not avoid hearing it all. He wasn't sure whether just to ignore it. He had heard Chloe behaving like this many times. Stephen did not shout back, and he could not help admiring him for his patience. But then it was Stephen who took control of the situation, much to Brian's relief.

"I am sorry you had to hear all that, Brian. My wife is suffering from post natal depression, poor girl. It's very hard for her."

Brian made sympathetic noises. It was a subject he knew very little about, as when Eileen had been alive, they had not had any children. "Can the doctor help her?" he suggested.

"He's trying to. I am sure we will get there in the end," Stephen said encouragingly.

"Meanwhile Chloe has run down the road," pointed out Brian.

Just at that moment Kay, the nanny, came into view behind Stephen, who was still standing by the open door. Seeing the consternation on Stephen's face, she said quietly, "I heard how upset

Chloe was. Luke is now sleeping, so if you like I can go after her and see if I can calm her down."

Stephen's look of gratitude was not lost on her. Brian went back to weeding his flower bed. After all, it was not his business, but he couldn't help feeling sorry for Stephen.

"Kay, I know it's not part of your job, but she won't listen to me. Another woman may be able to get through to her. I will listen out for Luke whilst you are gone."

Kay smiled back at him. She would do anything to help this couple. She had worked here for three months, ever since Chloe had brought her newborn son Luke home from hospital.

Kay was twenty-three years old, and had proved to be a very capable nanny. She was tall and slim, with dark hair which she wore usually in a pony tail when she was at work. She was not a great beauty, but when she smiled it transformed her face and made her look quite attractive.

She had not met 'the one' yet, but she had a very romantic nature. Before she had ever met Stephen she had heard of him. Stephen Ward, author of many romantic novels. She loved reading his books, as they always had very happy endings. Until he met Chloe, he was a confirmed thirty-two year old bachelor. His dark Latin looks would attract many women, and before Chloe became ill, Chloe had told Kay how they had met on holiday in Crete, and he had fallen hook, line and sinker for her. It wasn't surprising, with her auburn brown hair and green eyes, which were big and full of expression, not many men would be able to resist Chloe. Kay could not help envying her beauty.

That was a year ago. Chloe had fallen pregnant immediately, and Luke had been born in February, barely nine months after their marriage. But sadly, since his birth, Chloe had turned into a nervous, out of control person. She was under the care of Dr Richard Lyon, a very respected private specialist, who excelled in helping patients with mental health problems.

Kay's long legs soon covered the ground, and she caught up with Chloe. She knew exactly where Chloe would go, and she came panting up to her just as she opened the door to go into The Royal

Albion Hotel. "Hi Chloe, Luke's asleep, and Stephen has given me some time off. Can we have a drink together?"

Chloe was carrying a big secret, and it continually haunted her. She had lived in Broadstairs all her life. It had been just her and Daddy at the house in Stone Road, as her mother had died when she was very young. She didn't really remember her mother, but had seen photos where she was holding her as a young baby, which her dad had cherished so much. Chloe and her father Jack had always been close. He had constantly referred to them as being a good team, but she could sense his sadness at losing the love of his life. Her mother had died from a brain tumour at just twenty-six years old. A year ago, at the age of twenty-five, Chloe had come home from work to find her father dead in a chair; he had suffered a heart attack. Jack was just fifty-two years old.

This really knocked Chloe for six, as he had been both mother and father to her. She hadn't bothered too much with boyfriends. Being ambitious, she had set up her own business; buying a small local shop in Ramsgate and then turning it into a lucrative ladies fashion shop. So her life had revolved around fashion and home until then.

She just about managed to hold herself together to organise the funeral arrangements, and the wake was held at The Royal Albion Hotel, a place her father had frequented regularly. As well as going there for a drink, they had enjoyed many celebration meals too.

At the end of the evening, after all the mourners had departed, Chloe ordered herself a taxi. She was told that owing to demand, as it was the Friday of the May Bank Holiday weekend, none were available for at least forty-five minutes. She booked it anyway, as she knew she was well over the limit. Until then she had never been much of a drinker, but it was so easy, whilst accepting condolences from friends and family, who kept replenishing her wine glass, to keep sipping the wine, and enjoy the numbness which was temporarily masking the pain she was feeling inside.

The hotel was due to close now, so she opted to take a walk. Having spent all her life in Broadstairs, it always felt a very safe haven. She walked up Albion Street. The cool air felt good on this mild May evening. It wasn't even that dark, and as she headed to the promenade overlooking Viking Bay. She decided she would sit on one of the many seats up there.

As she reached the promenade, she noticed that the Bank Holiday Funfair was set up ready for the next day. There was just one man there, and he was obviously one of the fairground attendants. He was about her own age, with long brown curly hair, a very swarthy complexion, and sporting tattoos on both arms. He wore gold earrings, and his brown eyes softened when he saw her, and she noticed in an instant just how handsome he was.

"All right, love?" he asked, wondering what a woman was doing wandering up there alone at this time of night.

Suddenly all of Chloe's control crumbled. After putting on a brave face all evening, chatting to everyone, and trying to be strong for Daddy, she found herself in floods of tears. Then she poured it all out to this man, who had introduced himself as Vince.

"Come and sit in the van with me. I think you need a brandy," he said.

Chloe didn't think twice. He was a total stranger, but it seemed he had a heart. So she climbed into the van, and he left the door open. Vince decided a brandy wouldn't be enough, so he slipped a bit of something he thought would cheer her up into the drink. By the time she had finished it, Chloe was feeling very light-headed, and for now she felt she could park her grief, and she had an overwhelming desire to party.

Vince encouraged her to laugh, and after a while he shut the door and moved in to put his arms around her. In her grief, the feeling of being in someone's arms and being kissed was overwhelming. This man was so attractive, and before she knew it he was touching her gently, and removing her clothes. Then it happened, she had her first experience of sex in the back of a van with a stranger, and even a whole year later she could still feel shame for what she had done.

She had walked home after that, not bothering to wait for the taxi. Then she spent ages in the shower, trying to wash away her guilt at what she had done. The very next morning she booked herself a two

10

week holiday in Crete. She needed to get away, and try and forget what had happened to her.

On holiday she had met Stephen. Recognising him when he was at dinner, she had asked for his autograph. Then they had spent the rest of the holiday together, and she had found him so easy to talk to, and could share her grief with him about losing her father. Stephen was gentle and kind; a good listener, which was just what she needed at this time. By the end of the holiday, he had asked her to marry him, and she really felt she had fallen in love with him. Being with him would mean she didn't have to go back to an empty house. He had said he would sell his London home and come and live in Broadstairs with her.

They got married just two weeks after they came home, by special licence, and by then Chloe had suspected she was pregnant. After it was confirmed, Stephen was so happy, and he said it was the best news ever. So Chloe felt she had no choice but to let him think the baby was his. In truth, she didn't know if he was the father, or Vince, and since that day her deceitfulness had continued to haunt her. It was now a year since that fateful evening, and a compulsion to see Vince again, and tell him of her predicament, had brought her up here to the town. But she hadn't bargained on having company; the nanny would have to go.

"Let's sit here by the window, suggested Kay." She was relieved to see that Chloe seemed much calmer now, but she was going to have to make sure Chloe didn't get drunk. She had been discreetly told by Stephen that Chloe was drinking too much, which probably explained why she had found an almost empty wine bottle stashed in the cupboard under the sink in the kitchen. She had not told Stephen about it, but just poured the rest of the wine down the sink, and then rinsed out the bottle and put it in the recycling bin.

"OK, I just want a Diet Coke," said Chloe to her relief. So she went up to the bar and got them both the same, whilst Chloe sat at the table. Chloe was a bit wary of Kay, wondering why she had come after her. Recently a lot of things didn't seem to make sense, and she prayed that she wasn't losing her mind. Since Luke had

11

been born, Stephen had not come near her. He slept in the spare room, and as this had coincided with Kay joining them as a nanny, it had flashed through her mind that he might be having an affair with Kay.

"I am sorry that I got upset. Stephen means everything to me, but right now I feel exhausted after giving birth. Luke is an amazing baby, and I am doing my best to breastfeed him."

"Well, expressing your milk for times when I am caring for him is a really good idea," said Kay.

Chloe met her eyes. She couldn't fathom out whether Kay was sincere or not, or whether she wanted her son and her husband. Chloe really wanted to shake the fog that seemed to envelop her, and care for Luke herself, but right now her doctor had advised her that she needed the support of a nanny.

They sat there chatting about Luke for about half an hour. There was no way that Chloe was going to share her secret with Kay, as she had no idea if she could trust her. The only person she had told was Anna, who had been her best friend forever. She felt she could trust Anna with her life. Eventually Chloe suggested that they walk back home. She realised she would have to return this evening and seek out Vince. She would have to find a way to leave the house without Stephen suspecting anything.

By the time they got home, Luke was awake and hungry, and as Chloe was feeling more in control, she picked him up to feed him. By a miracle, even though her mental health was not good, she still had her milk. Kay usually stayed for bath time in case Chloe couldn't manage it, and left at six o'clock, but Chloe told her she could go at five today as she wanted to bath Luke herself.

Stephen was shut in his study, writing his latest novel, but he came downstairs to make sure she was all right now.

"Yes, I am fine. Kay is going home now and I am bathing Luke," said Chloe firmly, noticing that a look had passed between Stephen and Kay. Was she imagining it?

Stephen went to see Kay out, whilst thanking her for her support.

"Is she OK now?" he whispered, as he stood at the door.

"She seems to be. She suddenly decided to feed and bath Luke. She is definitely making an effort," explained Kay, as she started to descend the steps down into the garden.

Stephen shut the door and returned to his study. His mind was full of the story he was writing, and luckily Chloe seemed to have got over her fit of depression earlier and had taken charge of Luke. He paused at his study door. "Give me a shout if you need any help, darling," he said.

"I will, but we are fine," said Chloe, who was now running a bath for Luke.

Stephen felt relieved; now he could finally get on with some work. He shut his study door.

It was now after eleven o'clock. Luke was fast asleep in his cot, and Stephen had retired to bed in the spare room, complaining of a headache. This was Chloe's chance, and she took it, soon hurrying along Stone Road towards Albion Street. A quick look inside the bar satisfied her that Vince was not in there finishing a drink. She guessed his van might be parked up by the funfair, so she walked around to the promenade which overlooked Viking Bay. It was deserted round there, but then she spotted his van. He was sitting outside it smoking something which had quite a pungent odour. When he saw her, his face brightened.

"Hi Chloe. Want some of this? It really calms the nerves."

"Well I need something, because I have some really important news to share with you," she said, taking the proffered cigarette and drawing deeply on it. "You may be the father of my son."

Vince's eyes widened with disbelief. He had not expected this. Good God, it couldn't be true! His girlfriend would dump him if she knew, and he would never get to see his kids. He'd only slept with Chloe once. "I thought you were on the pill," he said wildly, not wanting to feel it was in any way his fault.

"No, because I didn't have a boyfriend, and wasn't expecting to sleep with anyone. But I am married now, and just thought you ought to know. It's been weighing heavily on my conscience."

"There is no future for us, I already have a family," Vince said desperately. "If you are married then your husband is his father."

"Oh, I know all about that. But keeping this secret has affected my mental health, and I just thought I should let you know."

Vince stared fixedly at her. She was telling him about a child which may or may not be his. Her husband didn't know, and all she was worried about was her mental health. He felt his temper rise!

Stephen woke up with a start, and he sat up in bed momentarily confused. But everything was quiet and calm around him. Luke wasn't crying, there was no loud music or car horns, and he presumed Chloe must be asleep. He went into the bedroom next door to check but, to his surprise, her bed was empty. Luke was sleeping soundly in the cot next to it, his little arms stretched upwards, which usually meant he was in a very sound sleep.

It was a warm night, so he didn't bother to find his slippers. Maybe Chloe was downstairs having a cup of tea. He checked the kitchen and the front room, putting the hall light on as he went, but his fears grew as he realised Chloe was not in the house. With trembling hands he picked up his mobile. It might be midnight, but he had to phone Richard; he would know what to do.

Richard Lyon answered his mobile very quickly. He was not in bed. He often stayed up late doing paperwork. "Yes, Stephen, what can I do for you?"

"It's Chloe. She's out in the dark on her own. She was upset earlier, but after Kay spent some time with her she said she was OK, and I thought she was."

"Any idea where she might be?"

"None at all."

"OK. I know you can't leave Luke so I will come over. I'll have a drive around the town and check the promenade, just to see if I can see her on the way."

"Thank you so much, Richard. I really don't know what sort of frame of mind she might be in. She was crying earlier, and seemed desperate to get out."

"Don't worry. I am on my way."

Richard Lyon lived in Ramsgate, and it was just a few minutes drive to Broadstairs from his flat. He divided his time between his flat in Ramsgate and his main apartment, which was near to his Harley Street practice. He was thirty-four years old, of medium height, with dark hair, which was always neatly groomed, and grey rather serious eyes. He always dressed smartly, and had many well cut suits to wear to his practice. He didn't own a pair of jeans, but favoured light off-white cotton trousers and casual open necked shirts when he was not working.

Stephen and Richard had known each other since they had been at university together. Their friendship had lasted many years, so he was now coming to help out Stephen and Chloe, not just as her doctor, but as a friend.

Stephen could not stop pacing up and down whilst he waited for Richard. Where on earth was Chloe, and whatever had possessed her to go out? After about half an hour, Richard arrived, running quickly up the steps to the house.

"I'm sorry. I couldn't find her anywhere," he said, dejectedly.

At that moment Luke could be heard crying. "Oh no, he wants a feed," said Stephen, desperately.

Seeing how anxious Stephen was, Richard immediately took control of the situation.

"I will lift him out and feed him. How about you pop round to the promenade. She likes to walk along there. I only checked the high street and down by the Royal Albion Hotel."

"Yes, I will. She has expressed her milk, and there is a bottle in the fridge. But if I can't find her, then we need to call the police," said Stephen. "It's getting serious now."

Richard nodded his agreement, and went to the fridge and found the bottle. Luke needed his feed.

Chapter Two

Sam Turner was eighteen years old. He had left school at fifteen because he was getting nowhere fast. It wasn't that he didn't have a brain; he coped with school work, but he didn't have friends. He was a loner, and an object of ridicule for other pupils to snigger about.

One day he flatly refused to go to school any more, and his mother Susan, who had struggled single-handedly to bring him up, after being widowed when he was a very young child, finally dragged the reason why out of him. He was being bullied.

Susan's first instinct was to march up to the school and complain to the headmaster. She had spent years defending her son in all sorts of difficult situations, and found it exasperating that so little was understood about autism, even though it had been properly identified as a condition where the brain is wired in a different way.

There had been a time, when Sam was a very young child, when he had sat on the floor weeping because he felt like the world was such a frightening place that he didn't understand at all; and for her that had been heartbreaking. She had been given the help of a social worker until Sam was fourteen, but cutbacks in social services meant that it had to finish, and since that support had been withdrawn, life had become harder.

Now that Sam was no longer at school, she realised she had to toughen up her attitude towards him, so she told him in no uncertain terms that if he wasn't going back to school, then he must find a job.

It broke her heart to lay down the law in that way, as she knew that the hardest thing for Sam, with his lack of social skills, would be passing a job interview.

Sam always took everything literally, so he had walked into the council offices at Margate, and told them quite frankly that he was autistic, had left school and needed a job, and quite liked gardening.

Bob Harris, who was on duty at the time, was quite amused by this novel approach. This lad was a fit looking youngster, well presented with short hair neatly styled, and the earnestness of his manner was quite endearing, as was his naivety. Bob had never been approached in this way before. They had just come out of lockdown after Covid had struck, and the parks and highways looked sadly neglected. What was needed were labourers who didn't mind getting their hands dirty or working hard, but so far there had not been many applicants. In the past immigrants had done the job, but since Covid and leaving the EU not so many had come to England. There was also the need to recruit anyone willing to work, and fulfilling the council's equal equalities requirements. A recent meeting had been held, and he had been informed that they must now employ a certain amount of people who had various physical or mental difficulties but were still willing to work, and he reckoned being autistic must be a difficulty. He liked the look of this lad, and he gave him a job as a gardeners' labourer on a three months trial basis.

That had been three years ago, and Sam had not let him down. Arthur, who was almost ready to retire, had taken him under his wing. Sam was a quick learner, and one day a week he had gone to college and passed exams. His job had given him confidence. Nobody teased him any more, and after three years he had qualified as a gardener.

He worked in the local parks and gardens. What he didn't know about flowers and shrubs was not worth knowing, and his proud mother could not quite believe how much he had come on. She was hoping that one day he might meet someone who would take the trouble to understand his unusual character. Anyone who did that would realise he had the kindest heart in the world, and he was always ready to do a good turn for anyone. Like any mother, she hoped that he would not have to spend his life on his own.

Sam and Susan lived in Kings Avenue, a turning off Stone Road, in a bungalow which was detached and had a fairly big garden, which Sam enjoyed taking care of. He had flower beds neatly tended, fruit trees which yielded apples and pears in the summer, and down the bottom part of the garden was the vegetable patch. Susan loved vegetables, and they were able to eat cabbages, cauliflower and runner beans straight from the garden.

On his days off Sam had spotted Chloe walking up and down Stone Road on her visits to the local shops. It really wasn't worth taking the car into Broadstairs from there, as one had to find an empty car park, and Albion Street was so narrow, you had to stop to let oncoming traffic pass. It was no more than a ten minute walk, so Chloe would only use the car if she was going further afield.

Sam had never found the courage to get himself a girlfriend; his life was centred around his job. In truth he had never been attracted to anyone until he saw Chloe and was blown away by her beauty. He knew she was married to Stephen Ward, the well known writer, and had recently had a baby, so all he could do was admire her from afar. He often walked behind her when she went into town; discreetly, so she would not realise she had been followed. He felt like his heart was bursting with love for her, even though he couldn't express it.

One thing about her really caught his attention. It didn't matter how hot the weather was, even if it was mid summer, she always wore a white silk scarf around her neck. In the summer it was tucked into her blouse, and in the winter she wore a long one, wound once round her neck, which swung back and forth when she walked. He did wonder why this was.

On this particular night there was a fairground in town, which had set up ready for the next day. They came every year. It would be situated along the promenade which overlooked Viking Bay. He decided to take a walk up there, just to check that none of the lorries had run over the flowerbed and destroyed the colourful display of flowers. He didn't really think about what time of night it was. Once Sam got an idea in his head he became blinkered to everything else. He did take his car this time, as it was late at night, and he parked it in the road, just opposite the ice cream parlour, then crossed the road to where the vans and lorries were parked next to the funfair.

He had brought his torch with him and it shone out as he walked along. Then he had the biggest shock when the beam of light hit the bench and someone was sitting on it. As soon as he saw the silk scarf, he knew without a doubt it was Chloe.

Detective Constable John Williams had been working as a policeman for ten years now. He was thirty-two years old and fit looking due to the fact he went to the gym as often as he could. Women found him attractive with his mid brown hair and hazel eyes, and he knew it. There was a certain arrogance about him. It had not prevented him from getting on, but it had not made him popular with others when he was posted to Thanet Police Station, which was smaller than the one at Canterbury.

He was a detective constable, and this status meant he thought he was better than anyone else. Of course, he did aspire to climbing even higher up the ladder of success in time, but right now he felt he was doing OK. He had a tough manner with suspects, and was inclined to think they were guilty without any proof, which meant that some of the other officers were uncomfortable about sitting in on his interviews. But to his credit he had managed to bust a ring of drug dealers in Margate only last year, and had been praised for his tenacity by his superiors.

John was single at the moment, having split up with his last girlfriend because she said he was married to his job. The truth was he had been getting bored with her, so had invented call outs and jobs he had to go to just so he could leave her flat in Ramsgate and go home. His home was at Westbrook. His house overlooked the sea, and had been inherited when his parents had decided to go and live in Spain. They could have sold it, but money was not scarce in this family and John was their only son, whom they had always doted on, so they bought themselves a Spanish Villa with its own swimming pool, and left the house to John. Visits back and forth took place, but John was very happy to live in the home he had always known since childhood, and when he had some leave, Spain was only a couple of hours away on the plane.

He was having a rare evening off, and had bought himself an Indian takeaway, washed down with a few beers, and by eleven o'clock was feeling quite sleepy. But just as he was getting into bed his mobile rang. He groaned with frustration as he picked it up. Whatever could it be? The voice of Carl Landon, who was on night duty at the police station, came over the line.

"Stephen Ward has been on the phone, sir. Very anxious. His wife has gone missing. I managed to rally a couple of officers. They have been searching all around Broadstairs, and then they found her, propped up on a bench next to the Bank Holiday Funfair. She's been strangled with her own scarf."

"OMG, that sounds horrendous. Maybe one of the gypsies from the fair has done it?"

"Not sure, sir. Local lad Sam Turner was sitting right next to her with her scarf in his hand. Looks like they had an argument. We have him at the station now."

John reacted quickly. He wasn't going to let anyone take over his case. "I am going to get a taxi right now, and come over to the station. Put him in an interview room and leave him to sweat."

"He's acting very weird, sir. Won't speak to any of us. Curled up on a bench, hiding his face."

"Well he won't be hiding his face when I get hold of him!" said John fiercely. "I'll teach him to go around strangling women. Has Ward been told about his wife's death yet?"

"He has, sir, and the press will be all over it tomorrow."

"Right. Hope I can get a taxi quickly. Can't drive as I have had a couple of drinks."

"I could try and rustle up a car, sir," said Carl, anxious to stay in his good books.

"I will ring you back if that is necessary."

"OK sir"

John clicked his phone off, and then dialled a local taxi company. They said a car could be with him in ten minutes, which was fine, as it would give him a chance to take a very quick shower and get dressed. He guessed that not too many people needed a taxi so late at night on a weekday.

Once at the station, he headed towards the interview room. Carl was hovering anxiously outside. "Right, PC Landon, I need you in with me," John said briskly.

Carl was not looking forward to this. He was aware that the detective inspector had a temper, and something about the suspect made him appear to be vulnerable. Carl had managed to find out he was eighteen. That was the only thing the young man had said. So he didn't need an appropriate adult, but after that he had hidden his face and curled up in a ball, which was certainly unusual behaviour.

"Yes sir," he said miserably, following discreetly behind John, who strode into the interview room.

John's eyes took in the youth, who was hiding his face and didn't look up.

"Right, what have you been up to?" he said grimly.

Sam was absolutely frozen with fear, so he did not look up or respond in any way. He just wanted to shut out this man's aggressive voice, and stay in his own safe world. Carl knew exactly what was going to happen, because he had seen it all before.

John's temper rose when Sam didn't respond. The insolent pile of shit was ignoring him, and nobody ignored DC John Williams! He would not put up with being disrespected! He covered the room in one big stride, and with his breath hot on Sam's face, he grabbed his chin, forcing his head up so he had no choice but to look at him.

"You ignorant little shit. You will look at me when I am speaking to you, and when you reply you will call me sir!"

Sam felt as if his insides were going to explode with fear. The feeling of terror inside him was so strong, his eyes were wide with uncertainty, and at that moment he felt so frightened that it had rendered him speechless. His silence made John even more angry. He put his hands around Sam's throat and barked at him. "How would you like to be strangled like Chloe was? You deserve it!"

In a bid to try and defend himself, Sam moistened his dry mouth and tried to speak, but as often happened in times of great stress, he stammered. "Nnnno Ssssir, didn't do it." Now the horror he felt at being a murder suspect hit him. It was all too much. He could feel a comforting mist enveloping him, and he slumped down onto the floor.

Chapter Three

Susan Turner was reeling with shock as she drove towards Thanet Police Station. To be woken up with a phone call telling her that her son Sam was in police custody, and had just been seen by a doctor because he had fainted, was a huge shock to her. She had no idea he had gone out, and believed he was in bed asleep.

They had not told her what Sam was supposed to have done, and she could not believe her mild law abiding son had done anything, but as always her protective instinct rose to the surface. She knew that he would have trouble answering questions. His social skills were poor, and if there had been any sort of bullying going on, that would explain why he had fainted. Sam had been subject to bullying all his life, but lately, since he had been working for the council, it had stopped.

She was ushered into an interview room by an officer who was on night duty. Sam was sitting on a seat looking totally bewildered and very pale. A tall man was standing opposite him. He was an imposing figure, and there was an attitude about him which she didn't like. He nodded at her.

"Mrs Susan Turner, I am Detective Constable John Williams. Your son was brought into custody a couple of hours ago. He was found next to the body of a local lady holding the silk scarf she was strangled with."

Susan's instinct was to put her arms around Sam and tell him it was all going to be OK, but the last time he had allowed her to hug him had been when he was five years old; it was his first day at school, and she had always treasured that hug. Instead she faced John and spoke fiercely to him.

"DC Williams, my son is the gentlest person ever. I do not know what you are suggesting, but I can assure you he wouldn't harm a fly!" Then, turning towards Sam, she gently touched his shoulder. "It's OK, Sam, I am taking you home with me very shortly."

John stared at her. She didn't seem to be in awe of his status. She was a small lady, no more than five feet in height, he guessed. She was probably in her early forties, and had brown medium length hair, which she wore straight with a full fringe. But what she lacked in height she made up for in character. The determination in her eyes made him realise she was not going to stand any nonsense.

"I am not sure you can take your son home yet, Mrs Turner. We need to interview him, and so far he has not spoken a word, nor been at all co-operative."

Susan became very angry at his words. This ignorant man knew nothing about autism, it was clear, but she was going to put him straight! She quickly took charge of the situation.

"Sam, just stay right here, I will be back soon. I need to speak to this policeman outside."

John didn't much like being referred to as a policeman. Didn't she realise his status? But he didn't argue with her. Susan reminded him of a bossy headmistress. She had opened the door, and fixed her eyes determinedly on him, and he found himself following her out into the corridor. Susan walked towards the front desk until she felt she was out of Sam's earshot.

"I don't know if you realise, but my son is autistic, he finds it difficult to speak to strangers at the best of times. Not only should you have contacted me immediately you brought him in, but also you should have advised me to arrange a solicitor."

"I am not interested in any excuses. He was at a crime scene with a body, and he was holding the item which had been used to strangle the victim."

Now Susan's temper rose, because this ignorant man was not listening to a word that she said!

"It's not excuses. You have broken the law. You should have had an appropriate adult in the room to support Sam. My son will tell me what happened in time, when he has recovered from the shock, but in the meantime I am going to report you to the chief commissioner, and, if I find out you laid a single finger on him, I will make sure you can't ever do it again to anyone else. But now I am taking him home."

All of John's arrogant demeanour had now deserted him. He had no defence against her anger. He knew he had not played it right, and being reported could cost him his job. Carl had seen him when he had lost it with the lad, and he was hovering in the corridor. In the meantime, Susan had gone into the interview room and collected Sam, who came out behind her with his head bowed. Spotting Carl hovering, she said bluntly: "Did you see him bully my son? Something must have caused him to faint."

Carl did not reply, but the look of guilt on his face was enough. He had thought John was going too far with the lad at the time, but he had to be loyal to his boss, so he kept his mouth zipped.

"Just as I thought! Your face says it all!" Susan flung at him. "You are corrupt, the lot of you, and I will see you in court!"

With that, she guided Sam out of the police station, leaving John and Carl speechless. Here was a woman they just didn't dare to argue with!

By the time they reached home, it was three o'clock in the morning. Susan knew now was not the time to question Sam. He had suffered a huge shock, so she packed him off to bed after making him some hot chocolate. He had not spoken a word since they left the police station, but in times of stress that was not unusual for Sam. After years of practice, Susan knew how to help him.

"I know you have had a nasty shock, Sam, and I am not going to ask you about it. But now you need to get some sleep, and when you feel better tomorrow you can tell me what happened."

Sam looked at her so gratefully. The man in the police station had scared the wits out of him, and then he had stammered, and he had wanted to curl up and die. He did feel very tired, and right now he needed to process the whole evening. Now that he was home in his familiar surroundings, with his mother, who had always been such a warrior on his behalf, it was better.

"Thanks, Mum. I didn't kill her," he said, and this time there was no stammer.

"Of course you didn't, and tomorrow you can tell me about it without any pressure," said Susan firmly.

Sam mounted the stairs. He knew he had the best mother, even if he could not express it. It would all be OK tomorrow, but nothing could stop the pain that was piercing its way through his heart like a bloody sword. Chloe had been his icon. He had put her on a pedestal in his mind and worshipped her, but now she was dead, and it was really hard to get his head around it. He quickly undressed and tumbled into bed. Exhaustion was wrapping itself like a cloak around him. He tossed and turned for a few minutes, but weariness finally overcame him, and he drifted off into a troubled sleep.

Meanwhile Susan had also had some hot chocolate. There were so many questions tumbling around inside her head. Why had Sam gone out in the middle of the night? What was he doing up on the promenade at that time? How had he come to find Chloe's dead body, and why was he holding her scarf?

Susan knew she would have to be very patient to get all the answers. The situation had to be handled with care, and if Sam was likely to need a solicitor, she would make sure she hired a good one.

As she climbed into bed she remembered that Sam had told her he didn't kill the girl. She had never known Sam to ever tell a lie, he had always been completely honest. So no matter how worried she was about him, she would cling onto that. She punched her pillow into shape, and then lay down. She was going to try really hard to get some sleep, and maybe when they woke up in the morning, nothing would be as bad as it seemed to be now.

b

Chapter Four

Alan Clarke gazed adoringly at the tiny baby nestled in his arms, and fast asleep. He couldn't quite believe that Erica was here now. Zoe had endured a lot of problems during this pregnancy, and with their son Adam now two years old, and very much making his presence felt, it had been tough.

During the last month, Zoe had been told to expect the birth at any time, so Alan had taken a week's leave just to be around if it happened. But the end of April came and went, then the beginning of May, so Alan went back to work. Of course, Zoe's pains started almost as soon as he had left for work, and not wishing to disrupt everything, Zoe had carried on as usual, dropping Adam at play school and then driving home.

Just after she had arrived home, her waters broke, so she knew the birth was imminent. That was when she wished that Alan was there with her. He would know what to do, so she rang his mobile. But Alan was in the middle of a team briefing and had left his phone at his desk. The constant interruptions of mobile phones often meant briefings taking much longer, and he had told his team to leave them behind whilst at these meetings, so he could hardly break the rule that he had put in place himself.

Zoe left a message to say the baby was coming and she was on her way to hospital, and then she rang her mother, who lived in Whitstable, to explain that she was going to hospital, but needed her to pick up Adam from playschool at twelve, and then take care of him until Alan came home.

Ruth dropped everything to go over. She planned to take Adam back to the house where everything was familiar to him, and then wait until Alan came home. It was such a shame that the baby had decided to come after he had gone back to work, and as Zoe had been unable to reach him, he might not even make it back for the birth.

Zoe had called herself a taxi. She wasn't sure she could risk waiting for her mother to arrive, and it was just as well that she hadn't, as when she arrived at the hospital her pains were much worse, and she found herself screaming with pain. Luckily the nurse who came out to meet the taxi had brought a wheelchair with her, so she was able to rush Zoe inside and straight into a side room, just in time for her to push Erica into the world.

There were no complications, and Erica was a healthy seven and a half pound baby. She was born at just after midday, and Alan arrived at the hospital at 1.30pm, half an hour after listening to his voice message. He was gutted that he had missed Erica's birth. He had been there when Adam was born, supporting Zoe, but it hadn't worked out this time.

"Well done, darling. I am so sorry I wasn't here," he said, smiling at her. Zoe was leaning back against her pillow and she looked totally exhausted. His heart went out to her. Women were so amazing. What they had to deal with, and very little fuss about it. His lovely wife had done him proud!

Zoe not only felt exhausted, she also couldn't feel a bond with Erica, and it worried her. Whatever was wrong with her? She had two beautiful children, and was married to the love of her life. She had everything any woman could possibly want, but all she could feel right now was a thick grey mist which was numbing all her senses. Alan was sitting right in front of her, cradling Erica, and the love in his eyes was clear to see. But she could feel nothing. Whatever was wrong with her?

She had wished many times that Alan had been with her, but it had all happened so quickly. He had really had to go back to work, but inside her she felt hurt that he hadn't been there. She knew she was being unreasonable, but she couldn't help it; she had needed him.

27

"You shouldn't have gone back to work," she said candidly.

"I know, hindsight is a wonderful thing," he said ruefully.

Suddenly Zoe dissolved into floods of tears. She had been trying to hold them back, but right now everything felt too much. Alan looked at her in alarm. Where was his lovely wife, glowing with motherhood? He quickly wrapped Erica in her light blanket and placed her in the hospital cot. Then he bounded across the room and put his arms around Zoe, holding her as tight as he possibly could until she stopped crying.

The comfort of his arms made Zoe feel a bit better. He dried her eyes gently with a tissue, and she felt calmer now. "Don't take any notice of me, it's my hormones," she told him.

"You are an amazing woman, and we are so lucky to have you, but right now you look tired, you need a rest. I am going to take some more leave starting tomorrow, and when you come home, I will be there to help you."

She looked at him gratefully. Everything seemed much better when Alan was there.

"I am coming home tomorrow; can't wait."

"Oh, wonderful honey. Ring me when they say you can come, and I'll be here in a flash," he said, gently kissing her.

"Give Adam a hug from me," she said as he was leaving, and Alan gave a thumbs up in response as he went through the door. Zoe leaned back against her pillow, hoping that once she got home she would be OK, and would shake off this weird feeling.

Ruth had been looking after Adam after picking him up from play school. She had also found some minced meat in the freezer, and was now making a shepherd's pie for when Alan got home. He had rung her and told her that Erica had been safely born, as soon as he knew. Although Ruth was longing to see her new granddaughter, she knew she would have to wait until the next day when Zoe came home. In the meantime, she had rung Gerald to share the great news.

"Will you be staying for a few days? You can, I will manage the breakfasts here," said Gerald.

"No, Alan is taking time off. I will stay tonight and come home after Zoe gets back from hospital."

The reason why Ruth and Gerald had moved to Whitstable was also their source of income. They had left the fumes of London to lead a new life by the sea, and now ran their own bed and breakfast business. Their terraced Victorian house in Whitstable was big inside, with rooms on three floors, which enabled them to take paying guests. They served a hearty cooked breakfast, and then the rest of the day was theirs, as guests went into Whitstable town in the evening where several pubs served an evening meal. They had made the move two years ago and, to their delight, Alan and Zoe had also come down to the coast.

Alan and Zoe had been renting a bungalow on the garden estate whilst they tried to sell their flat in Wimbledon, but now lived in Beltinge in Seaview Road. It was a spacious house, ideal for a family, situated on a corner, with uninterrupted views of the sea and Herne Bay Downs.

"I will take some photos of Erica to show you, and then we can pop back in a couple of days to see her properly."

"That sounds great," said Gerald, enthusiastically. To him all babies looked the same. But, of course, his beautiful granddaughter would be unique, just as Adam was.

After Ruth had ended the call, she put Adam in front of the TV. It was the time of day when he was allowed to watch it. Whilst he was immersed in children's programmes, she went into the kitchen to prepare the shepherd's pie. The kitchen was very spacious, and all the worktops and cupboards gleamed. The house had not long been built, so every room was immaculate, the décor was very pleasing to the eye, and the house was modern and light, with white painted walls, and fitted grey carpets everywhere except the kitchen and utility room, which both had grey vinyl flooring. Most of the windows had blinds, except the lounge, which overlooked a pleasant garden comprising of colourful bushes and shrubs. Velvet draped curtains in a rich shade of burgundy, held back with tiebacks, were quite a feature; they covered the patio doors which led out to a conservatory that extended along the complete width of the house. The conservatory had blinds in the same colour, and they could be closed when it got very hot.

She kept the door open, and kept popping out into the hall, then looking into the TV room to make sure Adam was sitting still, and he was, seemingly immersed in the CBeebies cartoons that he was watching.

Alan arrived about four o'clock, looking tired but very elated.

"Thanks so much, Ruth, for holding the fort. Our daughter is so beautiful. You will absolutely love her!" he exclaimed, bringing out his phone with lots of photos of her.

"Oh, how lovely. Now I can send some to Gerald. He wants to see her too."

Alan dutifully forwarded the photos to her. Baby Erica had white blonde hair, and plenty of it, curly just like Zoe; and memories of when Zoe had been a new baby came flooding back to Ruth when she looked at them.

"I forgot to ask. How is Zoe?" asked Ruth.

"She is a bit down at the moment; blames her hormones," explained Alan.

"Yes, that's what it will be. Didn't she have the baby blues after Adam was born?"

"Yes, of course, this is why we came to stay with you, so she wasn't on her own," said Alan, feeling relief inside him. It had happened once, and they had survived, so they should be better equipped to deal with it this time. He loved his little family with all his heart, and he didn't want anything to spoil the euphoria he felt right now, and the pride of being a father of two, one boy and one girl. When Zoe felt better she would feel the same, he was sure.

Alan went into the TV room. Adam stirred slightly, turning his head, and then a big grin spread all over his face. Here was the dad he had such fun with, the man who tickled him and held him upside down. He ran up to Alan, holding his hands out in welcome.

"Hello son, what have you been up to today? I hope you have been good for Grandma."

Adam could say a few words, but he hadn't reached the stage of putting them together to make a sentence just yet. He held his hands out to Alan, chanting, "Up, up, up."

"I know what you want," laughed Alan, swinging him up in the air until he was sitting on his shoulders. He then proceeded to crawl around the carpet pretending to bark like a dog, which amused

Adam very much. He started to have a fit of giggles, which spurred Alan on even more. Eventually he lifted the toddler down, realising just how tired he was. A sit down and a cup of tea would be really nice. It was almost as if Ruth had read his mind, as she came in with a cup of tea for him, and a drink for Adam, who was promptly lifted into his high chair so he could drink it without spilling it. Ruth also put some raw carrot batons on his tray, which Adam loved, and she knew Zoe would say it was a healthy option when he needed a snack.

"You and Gerald have been amazing. You have your own business to run, and here you are helping us out again," said Alan warmly. He sat sipping his tea, and Adam, who liked to copy his dad, also lifted up his baby cup and drank thirstily.

"Are you sure they will be OK with you having time off again?" asked Ruth anxiously, knowing how important Alan's job was.

"I can't help it if they are not. Zoe has had to play second fiddle on numerous occasions in the past. Many a time I had to cancel my involvement in an outing at the last minute, and she has always been so supportive. She has the baby blues at the moment, so I am taking time off to be with her and support her. I can help with Adam, and even get to know Erica," said Alan firmly.

Ruth smiled at him. They had always thought Alan was a great husband, in spite of his stressful job, and she knew if he hadn't taken time off, she would have come over to support Zoe. But he was such a family man too, and those two weeks with Zoe and the family would be precious to them both. She could go home tomorrow and know that Alan was taking care of everything.

"It will be a wonderful opportunity for family bonding," she said warmly. "Right, it's time for me to put the shepherd's pie under the grill."

Chapter Five

Alan spent the weeks leading up to the May bank holiday at home with Zoe. He turned a blind eye to any dust that had decided to settle on the normally immaculate surfaces of the furniture. His priority was to take care of Zoe, and also his two little ones. He played with Adam, enjoying the fun as much as his son did. Zoe was trying to breastfeed Erica, but was struggling. Then she developed an abscess on her breast, so the pain was too much for her.

Alan hated to see her so upset, and continually told her it didn't matter, and that baby milk formula was so good these days, Erica certainly would not suffer. So, because she didn't want to appear to be a misery, Zoe put a brave face on it. Alan had taken on a lot of the feeding of Erica, especially at night, because he felt Zoe needed all the rest she could get. He was incredibly proud to have a Princess, as he called her, as his daughter, and as for Adam, he was growing into a right little buster who loved fun times.

Alan had decided to return to work just after the bank holiday, but before he went back, he wanted to make sure that Zoe would feel supported. Being at home had shocked him, he had no idea how hard women worked. It was non-stop!

"We know Helen has her own work whilst you are on your year's maternity leave, so how about we get an au pair for the summer to give you some support?" he asked Zoe.

Everything inside Zoe was screaming at her to ask him not to go back. She felt an absolute failure. She couldn't even feed her own baby. Alan was feeding and changing Erica, and she still couldn't feel bonded towards her. Sometimes having a bit of knowledge was a dangerous thing, and having been a nurse for many years, and caring for patients with various illnesses, both mental and physical, made Zoe aware that what she was suffering with was more than just a touch of the baby blues, and it scared her. Because of her nursing training, everyone expected her to be a perfect mother. She wasn't supposed to lose control like this, but all she could see in front of her eyes was blackness, so dark that it wrapped itself all around her, and left no room for even a chink of hope that things might change. She didn't really want an au pair, as they would be living in the house, but neither did she want to be left on her own to cope with the children, so she agreed to Alan's plan.

As luck would have it, a nineteen year old French girl was looking for a summer job to last until September. So after they had both interviewed Monique, it was arranged that she would start on the Tuesday after the bank holiday.

On the Sunday of the Bank Holiday, Alan received a call on his mobile from Eric Cooper, who was attached to New Scotland Yard. When he saw his name flash up, Alan thought, surely they are not going to have a go at me for extra leave, so he answered it cautiously.

"Hi Alan, Eric here, how are you and your lovely wife? I hear you have a new daughter."

"We are fine, sir, yes, Erica is doing well." Alan was surprised at such interest. This couldn't be why Eric had rung.

"I seem to remember that a couple of years ago, in that case you dealt with so admirably when Eleanor Harrison was murdered, one of the suspects had autism, and you had to step in when he wasn't treated very kindly."

"Oh yes, Peter, can't remember his surname, but he wasn't very good at being interviewed because of his autism. Thanks to my partner Wendy Stuart, who has an autistic brother, we were able to interview him and exonerate him as well."

"Well, it's happened again. A detective constable at Thanet Police station has arrested a young autistic man and scared the hell out of him. His mother came marching down to the station and took him home, and has now made a complaint against the officer. He made a lot of mistakes: no solicitor or appropriate adult, and the lad was put under duress and fainted etc., etc,."

Alan knew what was coming next. He would be asked to take on the case to save Thanet police the embarrassment of a complete mess up.

"To be honest, we don't know whether the lad is guilty or not. He was found at the scene holding the scarf that the young woman was strangled with. His mother says he is gentle, but obviously you will have to interview him first. The crime scene was a wooden bench inside a shelter where the victim was found propped up, to all intents and purposes, just sitting there. It's not cordoned off now, as a bank holiday fair has been taking place. We took all the prints and DNA that we could, but it means little as so many people sit in that shelter. As for the scarf, it has the DNA of the victim, her husband and the young lad. Well, the husband's prints mean nothing, as living in the same house it's obvious his DNA would be on it."

"OK sir, I understand all that. Do you want me to interview the autistic boy?"

"I want you to take on the case. The officer has messed up. He lacks people skills, but your reputation of fairness precedes you."

"Thank you, sir. If I might suggest that I interview the young man at his home with his mother in attendance, he will feel more comfortable, and I am sure we can get to the truth."

"I am going to put all this in an email, and any other info you need. I am also going to issue a sincere apology to his mother so she takes it no further. I'll leave you, our ambassador, to deal with the case."

"Thank you, sir, I certainly will," said Alan. He sat staring into space long after Eric had gone off the line. What he liked about this job was all the challenges. Obviously catching criminals was the most important part, but restoring good relations with the public was also important. He was now impatient to get back to work and get on with it. His working partner and family liaison officer Martha worked very well with him, and he felt they were a great team.

He rang Martha to let her know he had heard from Eric, and was about to receive paperwork for a new case. Martha was pleased he was coming back. She had been assisting James Martin, but it wasn't anything very interesting; car crime was very common and it was hard to apprehend the perpetrators, so many got away with it. Working with Alan to try and solve a murder would be much more interesting and satisfying. She wondered if she was becoming a bit macabre. After a murder, many families needed emotional support, and that was what she was there for. For her, apart from the satisfaction of catching the criminal, being of support to a grieving family made her feel that she was doing her job properly.

"I have an email coming, so I will study the case, and then I need to set up a meeting with Sam Turner and his mother, possibly on Tuesday," he said, remembering that Zoe was expecting him to spend tomorrow with them. He had even suggested taking a picnic and heading out to one of the local bays. The weather was very nice at the moment. Then an idea struck him. He had originally thought of going to Joss Bay, where Adam could make sandcastles to his heart's content, but why not go to Broadstairs? Viking Bay was also very sandy. He might even be able to take Adam up to the top part where the funfair was on the promenade. He could then survey what had been a crime scene.

"OK sir, are we meeting at the station on Tuesday morning then?"

"No Martha, I will book in online and pick you up to go and interview Sam and his mother. We also need to visit the victim's husband Stephen Ward."

"Oh yes, he is a male version of Barbara Cartland. He writes very emotional love stories. I have read one or two," said Martha, laughing.

"Not my thing," admitted Alan. "So he doesn't dabble in crime then?"

"Apparently not."

"OK, I will ring you tomorrow evening and let you know what is happening on Tuesday morning. Meanwhile, I will forward the email so you, too, can familiarise yourself with the case."

"Thank you, sir."

*　　*　　*　　*

35

The next day Alan helped Zoe to prepare a packed lunch, and they also made up a couple of bottles for Erica. Zoe's abscess had healed, and she tried to feel optimistic about the temporary au pair starting the next day. For Alan's sake she put on a brave face, but the feeling of wretchedness was still inside her, and she vowed to do something about it, and to get some help from the doctor. She wouldn't tell Alan. He had a new murder case to solve, and if she told him he might feel he could not go back to work. She must not be selfish, because his job was important to him.

There were a lot of steps down to the beach, and Alan had anticipated this, so they walked along the promenade where the funfair was in full swing. Alan noted the shelter with the seat in. It was very close to where the funfair with its entourage was parked. There were dodgem cars and roundabouts whirling about, and a big queue of good natured customers waiting to put their children on the rides.

Alan debated about taking Adam on the dodgems, but decided not to mention it to Zoe, after realising that it wouldn't be safe. He was only just two years old, and very unaware of danger. There was no way of knowing if all the bumping from other cars might frighten him. It would be best if he waited until Adam was older.

After standing and watching the fun that was going on, and the excited shrieks from the children, Alan and Zoe moved off and walked along to the end, where it was possible to get onto the beach without negotiating lots of steps. There were many people taking advantage of the mellow weather; children paddling, some even swimming, toddlers running about with buckets of water to pour into the moat that had been enthusiastically created for them.

Being on the beach was what Adam wanted, and Alan couldn't wait to help him to build a few sandcastles. Zoe had brought a rug, which she spread onto the ground so they could all sit down. Erica was strapped to her in a baby papoose, and this should have made Zoe feel closer to her, but it didn't. This worried Zoe, but she felt too ashamed to share it with Alan, who clearly adored his daughter. Adam trotted along next to Alan, and when he got tired, Alan would carry him on his shoulders. They had decided against bringing a pushchair, as it was hard to push it along the soft sand.

Zoe got their lunch out of a cool bag, and was just about to set the picnic out when Erica woke up. Her little voice rang out angrily, crying loudly, which flustered Zoe, and Alan was quick to intervene.

"It's OK honey, you carry on setting up lunch and I will give her the bottle. She's obviously hungry."

Zoe felt so relieved. Since Erica had been born, she felt that she hadn't been able to give Adam much attention. He was still a baby himself, and she wanted to see him eat his lunch as he had not eaten his breakfast properly. She gently lifted her angry baby daughter out of the papoose and handed her to Alan. He rocked her gently, and her eyes briefly fixed upon him. Zoe handed him the bottle, and he squatted down on the blanket, resting Erica against his right arm, and guided the teat into her hungry mouth.

Zoe and Adam ate some lunch, then when Alan had finished feeding Erica, Zoe took her to wind her, and Alan ate a ham sandwich and a packet of crisps. Alan chuckled when he saw that Adam had eaten his finger sandwich, but used the crisps to line them up like sentries guarding a fortress.

"Dad's gonna eat your crisps," he said, poking him playfully, and Adam's response to this was to try and shovel them very quickly into his mouth. When Zoe was satisfied she had all of Erica's wind up, she quickly changed her disposable nappy, then got up, and walked over to a nearby bin to dispose of it.

Once back in her papoose, it didn't take Erica long to fall asleep again. Adam had finished eating and drinking now, so Alan found a patch of sand, and started to pile it into the yellow bucket he had brought with him. Adam became very excited. He built him a couple of sandcastles, and scraped out the sand to make a moat.

"Come on, son, let's fill it with water," he said, and with Adam trotting beside him, they walked out to the water's edge. Alan had his shorts on, so could paddle with him, and Adam had his little swimming trunks. He grabbed the bucket excitedly from his dad and dipped it into the water. Then he held it upside down, and laughed when the water ran out.

Alan was enjoying himself as much as Adam was. They giggled together, and finally managed to get a bucketful to tip into the moat.

Zoe watched on. It was nice to see Alan taking some time off and having fun with Adam. Tomorrow their new nanny au pair was going to start, so she would have some support, but still, inside herself, she felt lost. There was no need to worry anyone else with this, but she was going to get help. She knew from all her years working at the hospital, mental health was as important as physical health, and if it was ignored she would only get worse. As soon as she had some time to herself she would get some help. In the meantime, she put on her brightest smile, and addressed Alan.

"Whose having the most fun?"

"I am, of course," Alan quipped back, so pleased to see her sunny smile again. As much as he loved both of his children, Zoe was the most important person in his life. If she was OK, then he was.

Chapter Six

Monique arrived bright and early at seven o'clock on Tuesday morning. She had responded to an online advertisement, as the agency could not promise a match immediately. Alan and Zoe had interviewed her together. She had a strong and confident nature, and a calm manner. Not particularly chatty, but had already met the babies and seemed to really care about them. Adam had climbed onto her lap almost immediately, which was the main reason why they both thought she was right for the job. Adam liked her, so would be happy being cared for by her.

Although nineteen, Monique looked older. She wore her dark hair on top of her head, which made her look sophisticated, her eyes were brown and her skin had a slight olive tinge. Although it was only May, she had a golden suntan; she was obviously used to sitting out in the sun.

She told them she had spent six months with a family whilst the mother had been unable to take care of her baby, because, soon after its birth, she had fallen down some stairs, and broken her leg and sustained other injuries. Luckily the mother was much better now and able to care for her own baby girl, and both the parents had written a glowing reference, saying how much support Monique had given the family at a very difficult time.

Alan left for work at eight o'clock, and by then Erica had been fed and Adam had eaten his breakfast. Monique was going to take Adam and drop him off at playschool. Meanwhile Erica was asleep, which meant Zoe could take a rest herself, and then when Monique returned, she would take care of Erica when she woke up. It all seemed quite orderly, so Alan gave Zoe a gentle kiss, and as he walked towards the door, she gave him a bright smile, knowing this would put his mind at rest.

"Have a good day, honey. I am sure having Monique around will help."

"Yes, it will, and I hope you get on OK with the new case."

Zoe watched him through the window as he opened the car door and got in. Alan looked so smart today. He had a navy blue suit on with a pale blue shirt and a navy tie. His shoes were shiny, and whatever aftershave he was wearing was very pleasant, and it lingered in the air after he had gone.

She was determined to make an effort today. She had some help, and Alan must not be distracted from the important job he was doing. He didn't discuss his job with her, but she knew he had been put on a case in Thanet. A young mother had been murdered in Broadstairs, and he had mentioned that today he was going to interview an autistic boy who was a witness. He had asked Zoe's advice, because during her nursing training she had worked with autistic people, and apparently this boy had a mother who had fiercely defended him. Zoe had smiled and said.

"Well first you have to make a friend of his mother, which for you will be easy, and then interview him in his own home. He will have more confidence."

Alan took Zoe's word very seriously. During her years as a nurse she had gained a reputation as a hard worker, and someone that people who were not well could trust. She was kind and patient, the sort of person that someone could confide in. He had decided to go in plain clothes today. Some people found the police uniform quite intimidating, and he wanted to gain Sam's confidence, and then start to put the puzzle of Chloe Ward's death together with input from Martha.

He didn't want to ring Susan too early, so he drove into Canterbury to pick Martha up. It was very busy at this time, with lots of people going to work, and children travelling to school. Once they had crossed the level crossing, he drove towards Upstreet so he

40

could pick up the road that would take him past Manston and on to Broadstairs.

He continued on through Cliffs End, and continued heading towards Westwood Cross. Once there he pulled into the big car park by the shops.

"OK, Martha, it's nine now, let's see if I can set up an interview."

Martha nodded assent, wishing he hadn't parked in the shopping centre. It was always tempting to want to look around the shops.

Alan had been given a mobile number to ring, and it rang out without being answered. He debated about leaving a message, and then decided he would. A female voice invited him to do so. He took a deep breath, and spoke, "Good morning, Mrs Turner. My name is DCI Alan Clarke and I would be very grateful if you could ring me back." He then proceeded to read off his number.

"Well, what now, sir?" asked Martha.

"We can carry on to Broadstairs, to the house where Chloe lived. Her husband said he would be home all day."

"Oh yes, of course. He is a writer."

"Well I shouldn't think he's writing much at the moment," said Alan. "He must surely be a grieving husband. His wife murdered, and a three month baby to look after."

"Well, if he didn't do it. After all, the husband is always the first suspect."

Alan agreed with her. With many murder cases, it often turned out to be somebody close to the victim. Sometimes all it took was an argument that ended with violence. Whilst he was debating this, his mobile rang. It was Susan, and she did not sound happy.

"Good morning, Mrs Turner, thank you so much for ringing me back. I am so sorry to hear about Sam's treatment at the station last week."

"There is no excuse for it!" she said sharply.

"I totally agree with you."

This took the wind right out of her sails, as she was expecting Alan to defend his colleague. He had a very calm and soothing voice, totally different from the other man who had terrified Sam.

"If you think you are going to stop me from taking this further. . ."

"Mrs Turner, the reason why I have contacted you is because

41

Sam is a witness to the murder of Chloe. I do understand about autism, I have interviewed someone else who was autistic. This young man didn't have a mother to support him, but Sam has you, and I wondered if myself and Martha, my family liaison officer, could come round and collect his statement, with you in attendance, of course."

There was a pause whilst Susan digested his words. She was curious to meet this man with a soothing voice. Her one fear was that Sam would be arrested again, so maybe talking to him would be the answer. "You can come and interview him this morning. In about an hour, he is not at work today. My son never lies, and he said he found her. He did not kill her, he is far too gentle."

"That is exactly why we are coming to get a statement, Mrs Turner. So we can eliminate Sam from our enquiries."

"Right, be here at ten please," said Susan, unwilling to relinquish control of the situation. Alan smiled as he cleared down. She was a tough cookie all right.

"Right, Martha, whilst we are here, let's grab a coffee, and then after we must head over to Kings Avenue."

Monique had now dropped Adam at playschool for the morning, and she turned the car round to head back to the house. Erica was asleep when she left, but might have woken by now. Alan had given her instructions to try and make everything easy for Zoe, as it was so soon after Erica's birth, and she needed a rest.

Everything about this family was a source of envy to Monique. They had a beautiful house in Kestrel View, with a view out to sea, plenty of money, and two beautiful children. In September Monique would be returning to her dingy and dark bedsitter in the back streets of Paris. Alan and Zoe were such a beautiful couple. She wondered if Zoe was aware that her husband was admired by many women, herself included. He could have his pick of most women.

She was here, hopefully for four months, her bedroom was spacious and beautiful, and she was going to make the most of it. As soon as she met Alan, she had felt the charisma that flowed from him. But then, she reminded herself, the last time she had felt this way it had ended in disaster, and now she had absolutely nothing to show for it. She didn't have loving and supportive parents like Zoe did. She had been on her own for over a year now, and would be on her own when she returned to Paris. Of course, the ideal solution would be to meet a man like Alan, with money and a property, then she would never have to go back to that squalid bedsitter. She could get married and stay in England, and she might even be able to become a mother. She felt her eyes start to form tears, and she angrily brushed them away. She had two beautiful children to care for during the next few months. She would take each day as it came, and enjoy it. It didn't do to look back, only forward, and life was always full of many exciting opportunities waiting to be acted upon.

Chapter Seven

"Right, in you come, and let's get this done!"

Alan was surprised to see that Susan was quite a tiny woman. Over the phone her voice had been strong and powerful, so he had expected a tall well-built person. He held out his hand, and put on his most ingratiating smile. He had to try and break the ice.

"How do you do? May I call you Susan?"

She nodded her assent. He was so far removed from that awful man John, she started to feel more comfortable.

"This is Martha, my working partner, she is also a great family liaison officer."

Susan shook hands with them both, and showed them into a very pleasant room, which overlooked an attractive garden. A young man was standing inside the room, twisting his hands together, his head bent.

"What an attractive garden. Do you look after it yourself?"

At the mention of the garden, Sam's head came up. "I look after it."

"Sam, this is DCI Alan Clarke and Martha his working partner."

"OK." He did not hold his hand out to shake, but Alan had been expecting this. Sam then went on to tell Alan about how he looked after the garden, which is what Alan had intended, and it brought him out of his shell.

Susan was pleased to see the interaction, so she decided she would play hostess.

"Would you both like some tea or coffee?"

Martha didn't really want another coffee, having recently had one, but she knew Alan would have another one, and if any biscuits or cakes were offered, he was like a little boy at a birthday party.

"Thank you so much, Susan. I would love a coffee."

"Just a glass of water for me, please," said Martha.

Susan bustled out to the kitchen, and came back with a tray of drinks and some home made scones. Martha hid a smile, wondering how Alan managed it. He could surely charm the birds from the trees. In the meantime, Sam was explaining to him every aspect of his job. Once gardening came up, there would be no stopping him. It was his great passion in life.

Alan liked the earnestness of his manner. What this lad didn't know about flowers and trees was not worth knowing. He had clearly made a study of it all, and he could imagine that he probably did his job with great diligence.

After they had drunk their drinks, and Alan had eaten the home made scones, he was careful to compliment Susan on her excellent cooking, which brought a pink glow to her cheeks. She obviously didn't get praise that often. Alan faced Sam, and spoke gently to him, whilst smiling encouragingly at him.

Sam, I just want to ask you about last Friday. I am sure it must have been horrifying to see such a lovely young woman as Chloe was, and to know she had died. Can you tell me about what time you were there, and anything else you can remember?"

"Yes, go on Sam," urged Susan.

"I was in bed. Didn't notice the time, but mother was asleep. I knew the funfair had arrived."

Alan nodded his head whilst Martha was busily taking notes.

"Up where they park there are flower beds and shrubs. I take care of it and it looks very pretty, but when the fair comes they are not always careful about where they park. I went up there to make sure the lorries hadn't parked on any of the flower beds."

He paused at that moment. The next part would be hard to say, and he didn't want to end up stammering. Susan nodded encouragingly. "Carry on, son."

"There was a seat with a shelter close to where the lorries had parked. I had left my car by the ice cream parlour. It was very dark up there, but I had brought my torch with me. As I shone it, I saw her in the torchlight, it looked like she was sitting on the seat, so I went over to make sure she was OK."

"You thought she was alive then?"

"Yes, but her silk scarf was tied very tightly round her neck, so I undid it. That was when I realised why she wore a scarf."

"So why did she wear a scarf on a mild May night?"

"She had a red birthmark on her neck. She wore the scarf to hide it."

"I see, and then what happened?"

"Straight after me, a group of three policemen came. They told me off for touching the scarf; they said it was evidence. Then they took me to the police station."

"So let me get this straight, Sam. You thought Chloe was still alive, and you went to help her by untying the scarf?"

"Yes."

"When did you realise she was dead?"

"When that scary policeman told me at the station. He shouted at me. That made me stammer."

"You have done very well, son. I am proud of you!" said Susan firmly. She turned to Alan.

"You are very lucky. Sam is not usually a great conversationalist, but everything he told you was very clear."

"It was indeed." Alan nodded at Martha to stop taking notes, then he studied Sam more closely. He looked upset, although he did have his head up, making eye contact.

"I can see you are upset Sam, and I am sorry for the way you were treated at Thanet police station. Is this what is worrying you?"

"I am upset because she died. I looked up to her so much. She was beautiful, and she didn't need to wear the scarf."

Susan patted his shoulder. That is all he would allow, she knew, and her heart ached for his pain. Having a teenage crush, and then finding her dead, was truly heartbreaking.

"So you knew her, then?" asked Alan, but this time Susan cut in. She didn't want him to get the wrong idea because Sam did not explain himself properly.

46

"They live just around the corner from us in Stone Road, and Chloe used to walk to the shops. I have said hi to her at times, because everyone around here is very friendly. Have you ever spoken to her, Sam?"

"No," he said miserably. "And now I can't."

Alan could picture it; a teenage boy admiring a lovely woman from afar. No doubt he probably did have a crush on her, just like Alan himself as a teenager had been besotted about Eleanor Harrison. He could still remember how upset he had been to hear she had been murdered. By then, of course, he was in his twenties, but it had felt surreal investigating the death of a woman he had admired for so many years, and put on a pedestal.

He decided to change the subject. "Well thank you very much to both of you for your hospitality. I think we have all we need for now. If we prepare a statement, would you be able to pop into Canterbury police station, where I work, to sign it?"

Sam hesitated. He didn't like police stations, not after his experience with John, but this man had been so empathetic; he felt that he got him, and not many people did. "Yes, I can come over there tomorrow. It will be after five o'clock."

"That is fine, I will wait to see you. Others will have gone by then. It will just be myself and Martha."

Susan was amazed. She had just been ready to say no, it would be too much for Sam, but now she was glad she hadn't. Sam was eighteen, he was growing up, but over the years she had found she needed to be protective of him. Today he had handled the interview well, and DCI Alan Clarke was certainly a very nice man. Maybe she wouldn't bother to lodge that complaint any further. Most of the police force were decent people doing a hard job. But she wasn't going to tell them; let them sweat a bit.

"Many thanks, DCI Clarke," she inclined her head towards Martha. "Nice to meet you, Martha."

"Well that wasn't too bad, was it?" Alan commented to Martha as they got in the car.

"Not after you used your fatal charm on her, sir," laughed Martha.

Alan drove down and into Stone Road. The house was just a few

47

yards along on the right hand side. He could imagine that both the Turners had probably seen Chloe quite a bit. The house was tall, probably three floors, built in the late nineteenth century, with a flight of steps leading down to the garden. He noticed a Toyota parked outside, which probably belonged to Stephen Ward.

"Before we go in, what are your thoughts about Sam?" he said, turning towards Martha.

"I am not sure. Obviously his mother is very protective. He strikes me as not a violent person, although he clearly had a thing about Chloe."

Alan remembered back to his own past. It was so easy to jump to the wrong conclusion. He had also thought that Sam wasn't capable of violence, and his mother said he always spoke the truth. "Having a teenage crush is normal, it doesn't make him into a murderer, and I am not sure he had even spoken to her."

"As it was dark, he might have thought he could get it on with her, but she didn't want to. Wearing that scarf she was an easy target for someone who was angry with her."

"Well, let's go and interview the grieving husband now," said Alan, abruptly. He really didn't want Sam to be the culprit. He had liked his shy manner, and was impressed by his knowledge of gardening. He felt sad, because, if Sam was guilty, it would break his mother's heart.

Martha sensed that Alan wasn't ready to assume it was Sam, and she knew he was right. They had other suspects to interview before they could draw any conclusion. This was a very sad situation because Chloe was so young, and had only recently given birth to her first baby. That poor child was now motherless.

She followed him up the steps to the front door, and Alan pressed the bell. They could hear the echo of footsteps inside, and then a young woman, whom he guessed to be in her early twenties, opened the door. She surveyed them cautiously.

"Good morning, we are here to see Mr Ward."

"Is he expecting you?" she enquired.

Alan got out his identification, realising they probably didn't look like police. Martha was in a light summer skirt, with a pale blue tee shirt, bare legs and brown sandals, but he had asked her not to come in uniform.

48

"I am DCI Alan Clarke, and this is my partner Martha. He said we could call at any time today."

At that moment there was a movement behind her, and a man came into view.

"It's all right, Kay, do let them in."

A man came into view. He looked as if he might have Latin blood in him, with very dark hair and eyes, and a natural tan to his skin. Alan could imagine, after seeing photos of her, that Stephen and Chloe would have made a very attractive couple. His face looked sad, and although polite, he did not smile at them. "Good morning, detective inspector, do come in."

The crying of a baby could be heard in the background, and the young woman reacted.

"Oh, Luke is awake. I best go and check him out."

The hall floor had wooden floorboards. They were quite a feature to the house, as even when they went into the room with a couple of big old fashioned looking sofas, it was the same there, with just a rug in the middle. The walls were painted white, as were the ceilings, which were high, as was common to houses built at that time.

"Please sit down," said Stephen Ward, pointing towards the sofa.

Alan looked at Martha. He didn't want to rush this interview, as he needed to get an idea of what this man was like. So he sat down, and Martha followed suit, and then got out her phone, intending to record the conversation.

"Martha is going to record our conversation, if that is OK with you, Mr Ward?" Alan asked politely.

"Of course, and please call me Stephen."

His demeanour didn't change at all. He just carried on looking really sad. He really did seem to be a grieving husband. Completely lost without the woman he loved.

"First of all, I want to say how sorry we are that your wife Chloe has died. I wonder if you could give us an account of your movements last Friday evening 24th May."

"Thank you, I still can't believe it. Of course I can, I have nothing to hide. I went to bed early with a headache, and Chloe must have got up and gone out."

c

Alan stared at him, it seemed a bit unusual for a woman to go out late at night alone.

"So, let's get this straight, your wife got up and went out late at night. Did you have an argument?"

"I never argued with Chloe. She was suffering from mental health problems. Her father died very suddenly last year, and he was only in his fifties. Then getting pregnant so quickly. It had all affected her. I was sleeping in the spare room, and she had Luke in his cot right next to her."

"Was she having treatment for it?"

"Of course, I didn't like to see her like that. Richard Lyon, whom I know personally, has a Harley Street practice. He had been helping her."

"OK, so when did you realise your wife had gone out?"

"I woke up with a jump, but everything was quiet and still, so I just popped into the room to check if Chloe and Luke were OK. Luke was fast asleep, but Chloe was gone."

"What time was that?"

"I didn't really notice, but as I had been asleep, it could have been between eleven and twelve."

"What happened next?" asked Alan, whilst Martha sat silently recording it all.

"Knowing Chloe wasn't well and did unpredictable things, I rang Richard, and he drove straight over. He looked out for her on the way, but didn't have any success. Then Luke woke up, and wanted his bottle, so he offered to feed him so that I could go and search for her. When I could not find her, I telephoned the police, and the rest you know," he said very sadly.

"Right, so when you went out to look for her, where did you go?"

"I drove up to the town and looked around Albion Street, but even the pubs were shut, and there was hardly anyone around, so I came back."

"So you didn't think of getting out of the car and walking to the promenade where the funfair was parked up?"

"No, I was out of my mind with worry. I came back and called the police."

He held Alan's gaze without flinching, seemingly very sad and regretful. Alan tried to ruffle his feathers. "As you know, your wife was strangled with her own neck scarf. When tested it has your DNA on it."

"I am not surprised to hear that. My wife wore the scarf to hide a birthmark, which really wasn't that bad. I frequently helped her to put it in place. Sometimes she wore a brooch on it, but in this hot weather she just tucked it loosely into her blouse."

Stephen Ward was either a good actor, or he was innocent. Alan had to figure out which it was.

He signalled to Martha to stop recording. "That is all for now, Mr Ward. Can I ask you about the books that you write?"

"Well right now I can't write, but I write emotional love stories, and I always make sure they have happy endings."

His eyes looked full of pain, and Alan really felt for him, although he kept it to himself.

"So you have never tried writing a murder mystery?"

"No, never. I prefer to focus on happy themes. Dark stories are not for me!" he said firmly, and Alan sensed he had not liked the question.

"One more thing. The young woman who answered the door. . ."

". . .Is our nanny!" said Stephen, firmly. "Now that Chloe is no longer here, she has moved in as I need help with Luke."

"Well we would like to interview her too, before we go," said Alan. "And also your friend, Richard Lyon, we need his address and a contact number."

"Right, I will get Kay in, and then go and get Richard's details," said Stephen, and he proceeded to open the door, and raising his voice slightly, he called, "Kay, can you please come down? The police would like to interview you."

Kay appeared quite quickly, which made Alan think she had been quite close as he had not heard her come down the stairs. She looked a bit nervous, and he wondered why.

"Yes, I am Kay Wilson. I look after Luke."

Stephen excused himself and left the room, apparently not interested in what she had to say. Martha prepared to record again, and Alan spoke politely.

"I hope it's all right to call you Kay. Are you happy for Martha to record our interview?

"Yes, I am fine with that."

"Can you tell me where you were on the evening of 24th May?"

"Last Friday. Yes, well I finished work here a bit earlier than usual. Chloe had been upset earlier, but she was feeling better, so she sent me home at five o'clock. I spent the evening in my bedsitter at Ramsgate watching TV, but I don't have anyone who can confirm it. I live alone."

"Can you tell me what Chloe was upset about?"

Kay stared at him. How much did he know? She knew she must tell him about Chloe's behaviour earlier. As long as the police didn't get an idea in their heads that Stephen had killed Chloe. Kay looked up to Stephen so much, so she had to word her statement carefully.

"Well, Chloe had suffered with her mental health for a while now. She was devastated when her dad died suddenly. He was the only parent she had, as her mother had died when she was only a baby."

"Yes, Stephen told me about that, but what I need to know is what triggered her off on Friday afternoon?"

Kay wondered why she felt guilty about telling him. But Chloe was no longer here to feel embarrassed, and if it helped to find the monster who had killed her, then she must co-operate.

"I heard her shouting at Stephen on the doorstep in the afternoon, telling him to leave her alone because he didn't understand."

"So presumably Stephen got annoyed and shouted back?"

"No, Stephen knew she wasn't well. He never shouted or argued back, he had more patience than I would have."

Alan stared at her. Clearly Kay had a very high opinion of her boss, but was she telling the truth? "So tell me what happened then."

"She ran away, heading towards the town, and I came out because I heard her shouting at him."

Kay paused as she tried to reconcile with herself the fact that, no matter what she said, she was not being disloyal to Chloe, because she was dead. The police wanted to solve the crime, so anything she said might be valuable information.

"I offered to go after her, and Stephen said as I was close to her age, she might tell me what was wrong. He said he would listen out for Luke, so I went after her."

"Did you find her?"

"Yes, I caught up with her as she was going into the Royal Albion. We sat and had a chat, and drank a couple of Diet Cokes."

"Was she still upset?"

"No, she calmed down a lot, and apologised for her behaviour, saying she was still exhausted from the birth and trying to feed Luke herself. By the time we had walked home, she was very much in control again. She even sent me home early saying she could bath Luke herself."

"So when you went home, you no longer felt worried about her?"

Kay hesitated, although she hadn't told Stephen about the wine bottle, she felt she must tell this man. She lowered her voice. "Recently Stephen had told me that Chloe was drinking too much. I hadn't seen it myself, but when I saw her at the door of the pub, it flashed through my mind that she might get drunk and cause a scene, but she was happy with a Diet Coke, to my relief. A couple of days ago I found an almost empty wine bottle hidden under the sink, but I didn't tell Stephen, it would have felt like sneaking."

"So you threw the bottle away?"

"Yes, after I had tipped the rest of it down the sink. You see, the problem was, she was breastfeeding, and the alcohol would filter through to the baby's milk."

"So after you went home at five, you never went out that evening, and you never came back to this house?"

"Yes, Stephen rang my mobile and told me about her passing. It was awful. He wanted to tell me before I read it online, or heard it on the regional news."

Alan faced her directly when he asked the next question. "When did Stephen ask you to move into the house?"

Kay blushed slightly. "I offered, because until he met Chloe, he was a bachelor in his thirties, and didn't know one end of a baby from the other. Suddenly he is a widower with a young baby, so he needs someone to live in and take care of Luke." She didn't add that she was glad of any excuse to get out of her overpriced bedsitter, which had mould on the walls, and a landlord who never did anything about it.

"Thank you very much, Kay. If you could pop into Canterbury police station tomorrow, you can sign your statement, and also we need to take your fingerprints."

53

"Yes, I will."

Martha finished the recording, and they got up to go. Kay suddenly remembered the piece of paper Stephen had given her before he had retired to his study. She picked it up from the window shelf.

"Here are Richard's details. His mobile number and Ramsgate address."

"Many thanks," said Alan.

Kay showed them both out, and as they got in the car, Alan turned back to see she had already shut the front door.

"Well, she's got her feet nicely under the table with Stephen," remarked Alan, and Martha nodded.

"My thoughts exactly, boss!"

Chapter Eight

"Good afternoon, sir. The results of the post mortem have been emailed through."

"Anything interesting?"

"Well, apparently they have found quite a quantity of heroin inside the victim. She was very relaxed when she died, and didn't struggle when she was strangled."

"Where the hell did she get that from?"

"I have no idea, sir," James replied. "But I can forward the email on to you."

"Yes please," said Alan.

He clicked the call off and turned towards Martha. "What time are we interviewing Richard Lyon?"

"Three o'clock at his Ramsgate flat."

"OK, let's go and pick up some lunch. There is no time to go back to the station, but after we have his statement as well, I want to call a team briefing. Can you arrange it for tomorrow morning?"

"Yes sir."

"You also need to ask James to check on all these people to see if they have any previous convictions. If there is anything we need to know about them, I want it at my fingertips tomorrow morning."

"Do you want me to do that before I go and get some food for us?"

"I think so. We need to get on with this case. A motherless child; it's very sad," said Alan, briefly putting himself in Stephen Ward's place. If it had been Zoe, he would have been devastated. He was silent whilst Martha made the necessary calls and made arrangements. This job made you realise how fragile life was, and death didn't only claim old people.

"All done, sir. Everything is set up. Now let's go and get some lunch. There is a McDonald's in Westwood Road."

Alan liked the idea of a big Mac and some fries. He was hungry, so he drove towards the roundabout, and then pulled into the McDonald's. "Do you want to go in, or eat in the car?" he enquired, pausing in case he had to drive through and order at a window.

"I think I would like to stretch my legs, so let's eat in," said Martha. She didn't like the idea of eating in the car, as there wasn't a lot of room and it might be messy.

Alan pulled into the car park, and they both got out. It was an unspoken rule that they never discussed an ongoing case in public. Ears could be anywhere, whereas they could have thrashed out their opinions in the car. As far as Martha was concerned it was their lunch hour, which meant a break from the discussions.

They joined the small queue together, and when it was their turn, Alan asked Martha what she wanted. "Don't worry about me, just get yours," said Martha. She watched with amusement whilst he ordered his big Mac and apple pie, washed down with coffee. When it was her turn, she went for the healthy option; a chicken salad. Then a Diet Coke to accompany it.

"I knew you would go for the rabbit food," laughed Alan.

"Yes sir, and I knew you would want a big Mac, and I won't tell Zoe."

They both chuckled, as it was a standing joke that Zoe was trying to encourage Alan to eat more healthily. She usually prepared a packed lunch for him, but obviously not today. Alan liked to know she cared about his welfare and tried to look after him. He knew she was right, but just for today he could indulge himself.

It was quite busy in the restaurant, but Alan found a table by the window. They both sat silently eating for a while, and then sipped at their drinks. Alan then started telling Martha how Adam was trying to put his words together to make sentences, and the puzzling little pronunciations that he came out with which made them laugh.

"We all have to start somewhere," laughed Martha. She noticed how Alan's face lit up whenever he spoke about his children, He was such a proud father. As for Zoe, he adored his wife, and had expressed concern that she had to give up breastfeeding because of an abscess. Even though his job and career were very important to him, he had made sure to spend the first two weeks of Erica's life at home with Zoe supporting her, and risked the wrath of those higher up after already taking time off too early. Martha very much admired Alan, and his loving family unit. When Clive and herself took the plunge and started a family, she hoped they could experience the same sort of happiness and closeness that Alan and his family enjoyed.

After a while, Alan glanced at his phone. "OK, so now it's 2.30pm. We can take a slow drive into Ramsgate. Evidently Richard Lyon lives in one of the apartments on the hill overlooking the beach."

"Very nice," murmured Martha. It made her feel ambitious. She wanted to be more than a WPC. Clive was now a team leader sergeant, and they both wanted to climb up the ladder and achieve more. Then they could leave their modest flat in Canterbury behind, and maybe afford a house. She had been inside Alan and Zoe's new house. It was in a beautiful position, overlooking the downs that ran between Herne Bay and Beltinge, a beautiful spacious family home.

They both got in the car, and Alan drove slowly from McDonald's towards Ramsgate. They passed the harbour, where the boats were glinting in the sun. It looked peaceful, and then Alan took the turn which led up the hill. The apartments were in a terrace, with parking outside, although most spaces were taken.

"I think they might have parking permits," pointed out Alan. "We might have to find a side road to park."

"Or a car park," pointed out Martha.

The roads nearby also had yellow lines. Ramsgate was very busy, it was the time when schools came out, so after checking them out, Alan managed to find a car park near to the High Street.

"Right, we have to walk up the hill now," he said.

Martha didn't mind that. So they strolled up the hill, and at the top they reached the terrace of apartments with views of the sandy beach on the other side of the road. They checked out the number, and Alan pressed the bell. A voice came over the intercom, "Yes, who is it?"

"Good afternoon, Mr Lyon. DCI Alan Clarke and my partner Martha Brent."

"Please come in."

They went up the stairs, and when they reached the top, a man stood at an open door waiting for them. It was obviously a day off for him, as he was dressed in white shorts and tee shirt, his dark hair sleeked back with hair oil. He held his hand out to Alan in a friendly way, and they shook hands. "Can I make you both some tea or coffee?"

"Tea for me. Milk and two sugars," said Alan.

"Just a glass of water, please," said Martha.

Richard disappeared into the small kitchen, and they both sat down. Alan looked around him, and then spotted a photograph of Richard with a woman, and they were holding two small children, a boy and a girl, probably aged about two and three years old. He picked it up to study it, realising they knew very little about this man. Was he married, divorced or single?

Richard came into the room with their drinks, smiling. "That is my sister with her two beautiful children."

This answered Alan's question, so he put it down, saying, "Yes, they are cute."

Martha prepared to take notes, and switched her mobile on to record.

"Mr Lyon, are you happy if we record our conversation with you?"

"Of course, and please call me Richard."

Alan nodded to Martha, and then turned towards Richard. "OK Richard, it's a nice place you have here, and thank you for the tea. Can you tell us your movements last Friday, 24th May, in the evening, please."

"Yes, I spend some of my time here and some at my Harley Street practice. I arrived home for the bank holiday weekend at about four o'clock. I was looking forward to doing some walking, and also playing tennis. In fact I am having a game later on today."

"Do you belong to a club?"

"Yes, when I arrive here from London it's time to get fit. I also belong to the local gym."

"Were you here at the apartment alone that night?"

"Yes, I am not married. I live alone except when my sister comes to stay for a holiday with the children."

"Tell us about that evening."

"I had chilled out, and was in bed watching a late movie, then Stephen rang my mobile. He was very agitated because Chloe had gone out in the dark and he had no idea where she was, and if she was safe."

"What time was that?"

"I don't know exactly, but the movie started at eleven, so it was soon after that. I said I would come over, and on the way there, I drove down Albion Street. The pubs were now closed, and I could see no sign of her in the street. When I arrived at the house, Stephen was saying maybe we should call the police. Then Luke woke up and he needed a feed, so I offered to do it, so Stephen could drive up to the town and see if he could find Chloe. But when he arrived back he hadn't found her, so we called the police."

"Were you still there when Stephen received a visit from John Williams, informing him they had found a body which might be his wife."

"I was, and I am glad I stayed, as he insisted that he wanted to go and identify the body immediately, and I was able to stay with Luke."

"If you don't mind me saying, Richard, you seem to know a lot about babies, which is unusual for a bachelor."

"I have had plenty of practice with Margaret. She is a single mother, and I have helped her out many times."

"So, on the night in question, you did not see Chloe at all?"

"I did not."

"I understand you were treating Chloe for mental health problems."

"I was, but you know that I cannot break a patient's confidentiality."

This was a statement that infuriated Alan, but he expected it.

"The patient is now deceased, and we are trying to find her murderer."

"Yes, it's true, but all I can say is I was trying to help her work through various issues in her life."

"What about the scarf she wore winter and summer? Obviously her birthmark worried her."

"I was making headway with that. She sometimes took her scarf off when she visited me in Harley Street, and that is all I can tell you."

"We have found a number of fingerprints on the scarf, so we are taking everyone's fingerprints."

"Well, you can have mine too, but no doubt they are on there, as I often handed her the scarf and helped her to fasten it before she left the practice."

"Fair enough," agreed Alan. But it seemed the scarf was becoming a worthless piece of evidence, and would not be able to give them any idea about who might have killed Chloe.

Alan looked closely at Richard when he asked the next question.

"Can you tell us what medication you prescribed for Chloe?"

"Yes, a mild dose of Diazepam. I was working with her to try and reduce the dose and build up her self esteem."

"When the post mortem was carried out, Chloe's body contained a large quantity of heroin. It appears she had inhaled it into her lungs, but also may have snorted it too."

Richard's face became pale, and a look of disbelief came over it.

"No, that is not possible. She didn't even like taking pills, and she certainly didn't smoke."

"Forensics are certain," said Alan, calmly. Richard certainly looked amazed, or was he acting?

"Well she must have a dealer then. It's something I know absolutely nothing about. There is no way she should have been taking heroin as well as Diazepam!"

Alan nodded at Martha to stop recording, it was now time to go.

"Just one more question, Richard. I understand Stephen and you have a friendship dating back to your university days. Did that mean you should not have his wife as a patient?"

"It's never been a problem. She was part of my professional life,

60

and Stephen was part of my social life. We play tennis and go to the gym together, but, of course, it will be harder for him now."

"Thank you very much for your help, Richard. That is all we need for now."

Richard saw them out, still shocked at what he had been told. He just couldn't imagine timid Chloe taking drugs and smoking. He wondered if Stephen had any idea. Probably not, as he would surely have asked his advice about how to help her. No wonder her behaviour had been so erratic. It was too late to do anything about it now, but no doubt the police would tell him anyway.

Chapter Nine

"Well, what did you make of Richard Lyon?" asked Alan, as they drove towards Canterbury. It was now past four o'clock, so he planned to pop into the station, and then he could drop Martha home and hopefully get home himself by five.

"He was certainly gobsmacked when you told him about the heroin, and so was I!" said Martha.

"James told me when he rang. Something is not right. She surely didn't have a dealer in Broadstairs?" said Alan, puzzled.

"Well sir, they are everywhere. Even kids at school can get drugs these days."

"Yes, I know, it's a sad state of affairs, and we do our best to find the low lives that give it to them!"

Martha knew what he was thinking. One day Alan's children would be at school, and all parents wanted to do was keep them safe, no matter what age their children were. She decided to change the subject.

"I thought Richard seemed a genuine person, and he did seem upset at the mention of heroin. He went very pale."

"Yes, he clearly loves children. Not afraid to handle a new born baby."

"I expect some of his doctor training also comes into that," Martha reminded him.

"I can't see what his motive would be to murder her. He was trying to help her," mused Alan.

They had reached the police station at Canterbury, so Alan went to check his desk, and sure enough, there was James, waiting to fill him in on the recent checks that had been made.

"Good afternoon, sir, we have checked all the people that we have interviewed and none of them have police records. But interestingly Stephen Ward was declared bankrupt in the early part of last year."

"Was he, indeed," said Alan, thoughtfully. "So less than four months after being declared bankrupt, Stephen had met and married Chloe, who had her own house, and got her pregnant. A year later, she has had the baby, and her nanny moves in straight after her death. This is all looking very suspicious."

"Indeed, sir. Do you want to pay him another visit?"

"Not tonight. I will mention it at the team briefing tomorrow. You have done very well, James. Martha, you can go home now. Do you need a lift?"

"No sir. Clive will pick me up."

"I am off home now, James, but we can discuss all this at the briefing tomorrow."

"Yes sir."

Alan got into his car. It was going to take a while to get home at this time of day as the schools had just come out. But getting home and seeing his family after all these interviews would be so nice. He wanted to see Zoe's face light up when he came in, to know she was OK. He knew Adam would run up to him, and expect him to play immediately he came through the door, but Alan enjoyed the interaction as much as Adam did.

Zoe didn't feel as if she could make a friend of Monique. She was not sure why. Monique was polite enough, her English was just about OK, and she could not fault her. Adam loved being played with by her, and when she fed Erica, the little girl fed well from a bottle. Monique inspired confidence, as she always seemed to have everything under control.

At work Zoe had been capable of coping with any sort of crisis. It was part of her job, which she had always done with enthusiasm and diligence. But, right now, her confidence seemed to have deserted her, and she felt ashamed. Nurses were trained to cope with all eventualities, and because nobody would expect her to fail, it just made it all feel worse.

Alan was now pursuing a new murder case, and there was no way that she was going to add more stress to him by telling him that she felt like she was falling apart. So she took the plunge whilst Monique was out taking Adam to playschool.

Ever since Covid, it was really difficult to get to see a doctor. She could not go privately without Alan knowing and worrying, so she got on the computer, and did an online consultation. She detailed all her symptoms, including the fact that she could not bond with Erica, as this worried her greatly. By the end of the afternoon she had received a text back, with an appointment arranged for the next morning. This made her feel a little better. She could talk to her doctor, he was a kindly man.

So when Alan arrived home a little after five, all ready to help out with their son, she was able to greet him with a smile. Monique was going to bath and feed Erica, but Zoe knew that whenever Alan arrived home at a reasonable time, he would love to take charge of Adam, and give him his daily bath. Escaping all the baby duties for a while was a relief for her, so she went out into the kitchen to make dinner. She felt that was one thing she would not fail at, so it didn't take her long to make some pastry. A steak pie was one of Alan's favourites, and she soon became immersed in the preparation.

Anna Taylor had been friends with Chloe ever since they had started school together. They shared secrets and happy times together, and it was a closeness that had endured for over twenty years. Anna had curly blonde hair, and a bubbly nature, but she could also be sensible when she had to be. She knew what a close bond Chloe had shared with her father, and had always respected that. She knew how lucky she was to have parents and a brother. She also lived in Kings Avenue, on the other side of the road to Sam and his mother.

Chloe's whirlwind relationship, followed by marriage, had been a huge shock to her. She believed it had happened because of

Chloe's grief over losing her father so suddenly. Anna didn't feel she could trust Stephen. He had taken advantage of Chloe when she was in a vulnerable state, in her opinion. She could sense that Stephen didn't want her around. He wanted Chloe all to himself, and since he had come along, their friendship had never been quite the same.

When Chloe had admitted to her that she didn't know whether Stephen or Vince was the father of her baby, she just didn't know how to advise her. Vince had been a one night stand, and a huge mistake, with no future for either of them, but ever since then her mental health had suffered. But it just felt like Stephen was controlling her life. Even the fashion business that Chloe had built up from practically nothing had gone. Stephen had said she couldn't do that and be a good mother.

Then she found out that Chloe was seeing a Harley Street specialist, who happened to be a lifetime friend of Stephen, and it just felt like Stephen was in total control of her life.

When she read in the local paper that Chloe had been murdered, it was a huge shock, and initially she found it hard to believe it. Then her shock had turned to anger that Stephen had not had the decency to tell her, Chloe's closest friend. He had left her to find out in the most harrowing way.

The more she thought about it, she couldn't help wondering if Stephen was capable of murder. She decided it was her duty to Chloe to go to the police and tell them what she knew about Stephen and Chloe's marriage.

Alan was relieved to see that Zoe had a smile back on her face this evening. She had cooked him an amazing steak pie for dinner and he had been able to have a bit of a rough and tumble with Adam when he got home from work. He enjoyed it as much as Adam, because in truth it brought out the mischievous boy in Alan; he had never grown up.

It had been a good idea to have a nanny for these early days. After Monique had fed Erica and got her ready for bed, he had told her that her evening was now free, and he would bath Adam. They had given her a key, so she had now gone into Herne Bay to meet a friend, and return when she wanted. The weather was fine, the evenings were long, so she could go out and have some fun. It was nice to have Zoe to himself for a little while during dinner, and when he poured her a glass of red wine, she laughed and said, "Well, as I am not breastfeeding, I can have this."

"There is nothing like a glass of red wine to accompany this amazing steak pie. Nobody makes them like you," he said, smiling.

Zoe smiled at the compliment. She knew she had an appreciative husband, and she vowed to get the help and advice she needed to get over this hump in her marriage.

Alan was pleased to see her relaxing. She had looked tired lately. He was just hoping he wouldn't get too many emergency call-outs at awkward times, because right now she needed him more than ever.

Later, when they were in bed, he could hear her even breathing. As previously she had said she hadn't been able to sleep very well he was relieved. He kissed her cheek gently, whispering, "Sleep well, my love," then he turned over, and his thoughts returned to the case.

The shock of knowing that Chloe had been on heroin worried him. Where had she got it? It was unlikely that her psychiatrist would have prescribed it; no way! Then a thought struck him. She had been found right next to the funfair. Had one of the workers there given it to her? They might even have murdered her? The possibilities were endless. Tomorrow was the team briefing, so that was the time to thrash out all the scenarios. In the meantime, he told himself sternly, he was not going to allow this case to ruin his sleep. He turned his pillow over and settled down, tomorrow was another day.

Chapter Ten

Next morning Alan arrived at the station to find Martha in the office already waiting for him.

"Good morning, sir. I am so glad I have caught you before the briefing, as a young woman called Anna Taylor, who claims to be Chloe Ward's closest friend, wants to speak to you."

"Right, are the troops already gathered then?" asked Alan, grinning.

"They are, sir."

"Then I suggest they all have a tea or coffee whilst they are waiting."

"Yes, I did explain to them."

"Brilliant, Martha. Get your notebook out, or record what she says, whatever you fancy. I assume she is in the interview room?"

"She is, sir."

Anna was sitting stiffly in a chair as they entered the interview room. She looked as if she was on a mission, and would not be thwarted. After Alan had introduced himself and Martha to her, they both sat down opposite her, and Martha prepared to record her statement.

"Thank you for coming in, Anna. What do you have to tell us?" asked Alan, as it was clear she had something on her mind.

"Well, I am just trying to get my head around the fact that somebody murdered my best friend. I didn't even know until I read it in the paper, and also heard it on the news."

Alan was surprised. "Surely if you are a best friend. Didn't her husband tell you?"

"No he did not!" said Anna, bitterly. "Once he married her, he took over, and he didn't want me to be friends with her."

"So he was jealous of you."

"I suppose so, but he seemed to be in control of her, and before that Chloe had always been her own person. She built up her own business from nothing, and then he encouraged her to get rid of it."

Alan and Martha exchanged glances. This all sounded very interesting. Was Stephen a loving husband that Anna was jealous of because he had married her best friend? Or was he a control freak who had used her because he was bankrupt, and then taken over her house and her assets?

"So it's safe to say that you don't like him or trust him."

"I don't like the fact that Chloe changed after she met him, and was suffering from mental health issues. Even her psychiatrist was a friend of Stephen's."

"Yes, I did mention that," said Alan, "but he didn't think it was a problem."

"None of it sits right with me. The nanny seemed to be a bit too familiar with him, and not supportive enough to Chloe."

"So you think he's having an affair with the nanny then?"

"I didn't say that, but I do know what started off Chloe's mental health issues in the first place, and it almost felt like they were trying to make them worse."

Anna then went on to tell them about Chloe's one night stand with Vince, her whirlwind romance with Stephen, and subsequent feelings of guilt about who might be Luke's father.

Alan was trying to digest these revelations. This was big, very big, and a possible reason why she might have been murdered. "Did her husband know about Vince?"

"Nobody knew except me. She said she felt too ashamed to share it with anyone. But she did mention that when the fair came back again, she felt he ought to know that Luke might be his son."

"Right, well this is all very interesting. Now can you tell me what you know about Richard Lyon?"

"Very little, I never met him, but Chloe told me he is a gay man, he loves children, and when she visited him he was always very kind and supportive."

"OK, Anna, did you know that Chloe took drugs?"

"Don't be so silly. Chloe never even took a pill if she had a headache!" said Anna, scornfully.

"The post mortem showed traces of heroin in her blood. It was believed she had smoked it and inhaled it."

Anna went pale. "Not the Chloe I knew. I reckon Vince the fairground man must have given it to her."

"I reckon you are right," agreed Alan, "but the bank holiday is now over, and they have moved on."

"Yes, they move on to Dover. You can find the details if you search them online."

"Thank you. When did you last see Chloe?" asked Martha.

"Last Thursday. That is when she said she would try and speak to Vince if she could. I told her it might cause even more trouble, but I knew she would do it anyway."

"Can we talk about the birthmark on her neck, and the fact that she wore a scarf?"

"Well, you only have to look at a photo of Chloe to see just how beautiful she was, but it did affect her confidence. It wasn't that noticeable, just a red port wine stain, maybe the size of a two pound coin. If she wore a blouse you couldn't see it. In the winter she wore polo necks, and in the summer she wore a light nylon scarf tucked into the neck of whatever she was wearing. I always remember that at school she wore a skirt and blouse all through the summer term, not a summer dress, because they wouldn't allow her to wear the scarf. In her mind it was huge, but she was a bit obsessive about it."

Alan guessed that Chloe had obviously been teased about it by other children.

"Anna, did Chloe drink?"

"I never saw her have more than the odd glass of wine on her birthday or at Christmas."

Alan remembered that Kay the nanny had told him she found an almost empty bottle of wine in the kitchen, but had not told Stephen. He wondered who was telling the truth.

"Thank you so much for all your information, Anna."

"I know that Chloe is not here now, and if she was, I would never have told you, but could you keep the information I gave you about Luke private?"

"Don't worry, we have no reason to upset the family of someone who is no longer here to defend herself," said Alan, reassuringly.

After she had gone, Alan turned to Martha. "I think we should go and interview this Vince before we have a team briefing. I need to present all the suspects, and he definitely sounds like one."

"I was thinking that, and I was also wondering if that story about Chloe's fling was even true if no one else knows. Was Anna jealous because she lost her best friend, so to denigrate Stephen makes her feel better?"

"Another possibility to think about. In the meantime, if you can set up the meeting with Vince and check out the exact location, I will go and inform the team that we are postponing the briefing until we have information about one more suspect.

An hour later, Alan and Martha were sitting opposite Vince in an almost empty transport cafe. There was just one other person in there, and he was right up the other end, and out of earshot. Alan studied Vince, noting his long untidy hair; he looked a typical fairground gypsy. He was dressed in jeans and a tee shirt, and although young, his fingers bore traces of nicotine stains. He was not exactly oozing self confidence, indeed his expression was one of wariness, as if not knowing exactly what to expect.

When Vince had heard about Chloe's death on the news, he felt sorry that he had lost his temper with her the last time they had met. She had been a posh bird, way out of his league, and it had been fun, but to tell him that he might be the father of her child had really rocked him. He had enough trouble with Lena, his girlfriend, and they had two sprogs of their own, so all he had wanted the silly cow to do, was go back to her husband and play happy families. Looking at this policeman now, he had no idea whether he knew about that conversation or not, so he would just have to wait for the questions, and then answer them as best he could.

Thank you for talking to us, Mr Mulligan. May I call you Vince?"

"Yes."

"Chloe Ward was married to the writer Stephen Ward, and she was found dead last Friday night on a covered park bench right close to where your van was parked during the Bank Holiday Funfair."

The way he said it made Vince feel guilty. He wasn't accusing him, but it was probably best to admit he knew Chloe. If he was found out to be lying, they could pin anything on him.

"Yes, I already know about it. Initially the area was cordoned off, and then the newspapers were full of it."

"And you knew Chloe."

Vince was aware of Alan's eyes boring into him. He wasn't asking him if he knew, he was telling him that he knew, that Vince did know her. Vince had been a practised liar all his life, it had got him out of many sticky situations, but something about this man made it much harder to lie. He seemed to be one step ahead all the time, which was really annoying.

"I met up with her in 2023. Her father died suddenly, and she was very upset. She walked up to where my van was parked, and told me all about it."

"Why would a complete stranger tell you such a personal thing?"

"She had been in the Royal Albion at his wake, and had a lot to drink, and was very upset."

"So what did you do?"

"I gave her a brandy to calm her nerves."

"And what else!" barked Alan, angrily.

"Nothing else, guv." Vince could see that Alan didn't believe him.

"I suggest you smoked heroin, and gave her some, too."

"No guv, it's not true. I just have a little bit of weed sometimes to calm me nerves. Never touched heroin in ma life."

Now Vince was getting worried, this was not going well at all. Alan's next words took him completely by surprise.

"In 2023 you had a one night stand with her, and she got married to someone else. On 24th May this year she came to find you and tell you she wasn't sure if the baby might be yours. Did she find you?"

71

Vince found himself caught, just like a rat in a trap. Lying would make it worse. He would be found out. "Yes, she found me, and told me, and I said we had no future. I wanted her to go back to her husband. I was scared Lena would find out."

"Your partner?"

"Yes, we have two little uns, and she was looking after them in the caravan."

"So the mother of your children is looking after them in a caravan, while meanwhile you are having brandy and sex in the back of your van!" said Alan, contemptuously.

"I never drink the brandy when I am driving, guv, only when the van is parked."

"Oh, that is all right then!" said Alan, sarcastically.

He certainly looked very shifty, and his face was full of guilt, but was it because his one night stand was known about? Was this man capable of murdering Chloe?

"We need to take your fingerprints, so you will have to go to your local station and sort that immediately!"

"I will, guv, but honest I didn't hurt her, I wouldn't."

"If they are on that scarf you are in trouble!" said Alan, ominously.

Vince remembered that he had touched the scarf and made a threatening gesture to shut her up when she was getting hysterical. He hadn't meant anything by it, but his prints would be on it. He tried to think clearly.

"I will do whatever you say, but she had got her scarf into a knot she could not undo. All I did was help her to tie it more loosely, as she liked to hide her birthmark."

Not another one. Alan knew he had to concede the scarf was useless, it had the prints of everyone on it. Nevertheless, they had to follow the usual protocol.

"So what time did you see Chloe on the 24th?"

"It was late, just after the pub had closed. I came back to get my phone, had left it in the van, and she was sitting on the bench, the covered over one."

"Do you think she had been drinking?"

"No, not this time. She had stuff on her mind, as I said."

"So you gave her some heroin to calm her down."

"I told you, I have never taken heroin. My guilty pleasure is a little bit of weed sometimes."

Alan looked him straight in the face. "So you won't mind if my officers search your van and the caravan you live in?"

"There is nothing in the caravan. I wouldn't leave anything near to where my babes are. You can certainly search the van, you will find a bit of weed."

"We are searching both!" said Alan, angrily.

"How do I explain it to Lena? Please, no, guv."

"That's your problem," said Alan, harshly. Martha could see he was annoyed. "I am trying to solve a murder. Now tell me how Chloe was when you last saw her."

Vince had a momentary image of her scared face because he had been angry. He should not have grabbed her scarf, he knew that.

"She shared a few puffs of my weed, and then said she was going home. I got my phone out of the van, and left her quietly sitting on the seat."

"So who gave her the heroin then?"

"On my life, guv, it weren't me!" said Vince, desperately. And because he could not definitely prove otherwise, Alan had no choice but to let him go.

d

Chapter Eleven

"Let's get this team briefing done right now," said Alan. He had all the statements printed out and in a folder. Martha had taken care of that. He entered the room and strode towards the board at the other end. Photos of everyone they had interviewed had been pinned up there already. Martha was great, she was a liaison officer and secretary all rolled into one, he thought to himself.

"Thanks, you've organised it all," he said, smiling warmly at her.

James and the rest of the officers were all standing by the board, waiting for Alan to proceed.

"Before we start, sir, searches have been made at the homes of all the witnesses, and no heroin has been found. However, cannabis was found in the van belonging to Vince Mulligan."

"Yes, we expected that," said Alan, grimly. He wondered who had supplied the heroin. It was easy to blame the gypsy, but without the evidence there was no proof.

Firstly he pointed to a photograph of Chloe, and right next to her was a photo of the white silk scarf. "Let's talk about the victim first. Chloe had lived in Stone Road, Broadstairs all of her life with her father, as her mother died when she was a small baby."

"Was she an only child?" asked James.

"She was, and please note everyone, anything that I tell you about Chloe is strictly confidential and must not be shared with anyone outside this room, especially her husband, as it can only cause even more grief."

They all looked expectantly at him, knowing something big was coming.

"Chloe had a close friend called Anna, with whom she shared everything. I will speak more about Anna later. Chloe did well for herself in life, she bought a shop and turned it into her own fashion business. Chloe had one hang up; she hated her birthmark, and wore a scarf to hide it, although many people felt it wasn't that bad and didn't detract from her natural beauty. Then, last year, she came home to find her father dead in a chair. He was only fifty-two, and she was devastated."

All eyes were fixed on Alan as he continued: "She arranged his wake at the Royal Albion Hotel, and by the end of the evening, she had, unusually for her, drank many glasses of wine. She went for a walk in the cool night air, probably to try and sober up, and met him, Vince Mulligan, a travelling gypsy from the funfair."

He pointed at Vince's picture. "When interviewed, this man said she was upset, so he poured her a brandy, kept in his van, I might add." He could not hide the annoyance in his voice.

"Then he smoked some pot, and shared the cigarette with her. He said it was to calm her nerves."

"Any excuse," muttered James.

"Exactly, James. After that, apparently they had sex in the back of the van. Chloe went home, but was so ashamed of the way she had behaved, she booked herself a holiday in Crete, where she met Stephen Ward her husband. They married soon after they got home, and Stephen came to live with her in Broadstairs. Barely nine months later, her son Luke was born."

"Excuse me, sir, how do you know about the one night stand?" asked James, who was puzzled.

"Anna reckons that Chloe told her in confidence. But, when I interviewed Vince, I accused him of it and he did not deny it." He paused to take another breath.

"Now we go on to this year. Chloe has been suffering from mental health problems, and her specialist is Richard Lyon, friend of her husband Stephen. Her guilt over not knowing who was the father of her baby Luke is the reason she goes up to find Vince, as she feels he should know. She tells him, and his story is, after sharing some cannabis together, he leaves her sitting happily on the seat after they both agree there is no future for them."

"Do you believe him?" queried James.

"To be honest, he is the most likely of the witnesses to have done it. He was desperate to keep it from his girlfriend, and he also gave her drugs. Chloe's body had traces of heroin in it. He was the most likely person to have contacts, but nothing except cannabis, which he had already admitted to, was found on him."

At that moment there was a tap on the door, and a uniformed constable handed James a piece of paper. "The other information you wanted, James."

"Thank you," said James. He scanned it quickly, and then turned towards Alan.

"The background check on Vince Mulligan has been done. He has two convictions for being in possession of cannabis, one in 2021, and then again in 2022. He also has another conviction for being drunk and disorderly, and attacking a man in a night club in 2019, for which he served time."

"Really, that is very interesting," said Alan. We will come back to him later, when I have covered the other witnesses."

Alan took the paper from James, and added it to the file.

He walked up to the board, and pointed at the picture of Sam. "Sam Turner, an eighteen year old autistic boy, who is the reason I have this case, but that is another story. He was found sitting next to the body holding the scarf. He maintains he noticed it looked tight around her neck, and was about to help her to untie it. It was night time, of course, and only seen by torchlight.

"Do you believe him?"

"I do, his mother says he never lies, and he told her he did not hurt Chloe. Because of his autism, he finds it difficult to interact socially, but he knew her and admired her, but had never actually spoken to her."

"His mother is very protective, because she has had to be, but she insists he is very gentle, and hasn't got it in him," explained Martha.

"Did he have a reason to be there so late at night?" asked James.

"Yes, he's a gardener for the council. Loves his work, and wanted to make sure that none of the vans and lorries up there had parked on any of the flowerbeds that he takes care of."

"But why at that time of night?" persisted James

"I thought that," agreed Alan, "but his mother has explained to me that it's all part of Sam's autism. Once he gets an idea in his head, it has to be acted on immediately, no matter whether it's night or day, it's the way his brain is wired."

"His mother was not happy when we searched their house, but I explained it was normal procedure," explained James.

"Yes, we have to be really careful with them. She has already threatened to report someone who gave Sam a hard time. Of course, his mother could be lying to protect her son."

"Right, whose next then?" asked James.

"Have any of you heard of Stephen Ward, writer of romantic fiction?"

There were murmurs of agreement. "He is Chloe's husband. Been married a year, with a baby son who he believes is his. Appeared very sad and devastated when we went to speak to him. However, as soon as his wife died, the daytime nanny moved in. And apparently he was declared bankrupt earlier last year, but obviously, since her death, now has Chloe's house."

"Interesting," murmured James, "and the nanny?"

"Her name is Kay Wilson. She arrived as soon as the baby was born. When interviewed it was clear she holds her boss in high regard. She also told us that Chloe had been secretly drinking, even though she was breastfeeding, whereas Anna told us that Chloe wasn't much of a drinker. But, of course, Chloe did drink when she was with Vince."

"I think Stephen is another possible suspect. A nanny appears from nowhere, and moves in after Chloe dies. Maybe he wants a new life with her?" suggested Martha.

"Possibly," agreed Alan. "In the meantime, here is Richard Lyon, Harley Street professional, who was treating Chloe for her mental health problems. Denies prescribing anything other than a mild dose of diazepam for her and knows nothing about the heroin, he says. He is thirty-four years old, loves children and is a gay man."

"Well there's another suspect," said James. "He fancies his best friend, so bumps off his wife so they can live happily ever after." He grinned. "I'm joking, of course," and everyone laughed.

"So Anna stated that Chloe's mental health had declined, and she had changed since she was married to Stephen. I wasn't sure if the story she had told me about Chloe confiding in her about not knowing which man was her baby's father was true, but after confronting Vince, it was. She said she was worried that Stephen was trying to control Chloe. We are talking about coercive control, mind games, ruining her confidence, and maybe the nanny was involved."

"That is horrible. Those sort of men are vile!" said Martha, angrily.

"But can we be sure it's true?" asked Alan. "It was clear that Anna didn't like Stephen; he had stolen her best friend."

"Well, he didn't even bother to tell her that Chloe had died," Martha reminded him.

"Yes, that was not nice for her to find out from the media. I can understand she was upset. If Stephen is a sensitive, caring man, which he would have us believe, he would not treat her like that. So I think we should visit him again, and also, James, can you get Vince Mulligan in for further questioning. We have got him on cannabis charges, and there might even be more we can charge him with."

"Right, sir," said James.

"In wrapping up this briefing, not one of these witnesses has a safe alibi that can be corroborated by anyone else. Indeed, three of them were wandering around Broadstairs at the time of her death, and the silk scarf has just about everyone's prints on it, so we have to look for something more. Thanks for your time everyone. If anyone thinks of anything new or relevant, let myself or Martha know."

Having said all that, Alan turned on his heel and left the room.

Anna sat reading the card with disbelief. It was handwritten in beautiful fancy handwriting. She could not remember the last time she had received a handwritten card. Nowadays it was either a text message or an email. It was a beautiful handmade card with a picture of a lily gracing the front of it.

Dear Anna,

I wanted to let you know your dearest friend, and my beloved Chloe, passed away on 24th May. You may have already heard this, and I apologise for not contacting you by email, phone call or text. The truth was I am so devastated at her loss, and have struggled to accept it.

As you know Chloe had no family left, but you are like family, and I am hoping you will support me in honouring her memory when I make her funeral arrangements.

With kindest regards.

Stephen.

Now she felt riddled with guilt. If she was honest with herself, she had been jealous of Stephen as soon as she met him, because she felt he had come between herself and Chloe. It had been easy to think the worst of him, as he had taken over her best friend, and easy to blame him for Chloe's mental health problems, when, in fact, Chloe's own behaviour had contributed to her mental health problems.

He had laid his heart bare in that beautiful card, and he wanted her at the funeral service, so Anna felt it was only right to inform the police that she had maybe misjudged Stephen, and he was not a bad man. She had been given a number to call if she had any more information, so she rang the mobile number. It went into voice mail, so she explained about the card, and how she may have been hasty in her judgement about Stephen, and then clicked off.

Later the call was picked up by Martha. After listening intently, she made notes, and saved it, so she could refer back to it if she needed to. Time to inform Alan. "Just picked up a voicemail from Anna, sir. She has had a handwritten card from Stephen telling her about Chloe's death, and he has invited her to join him at the funeral. She has certainly changed her tune about him. She's now saying that he's not a bad person."

"How can we trust these people when they keep vacillating?" asked Alan. "Come on, that's enough for one day, we have homes to go to."

Chapter Twelve

"Richard, I really want to give my beautiful wife the send off that she deserves, but I have a bit of a cash flow problem at the moment."

Richard smiled to himself at the other end of the phone. It had always been like that; Stephen and money were always soon parted. Luckily his own financial position meant that paying for Chloe's funeral would barely cause a ripple in his finances. Stephen would vow to pay him back as soon as his situation improved, but he wasn't holding his breath. This was the only thing that had cast a shadow over their relationship in years past, but it would not affect them now. Richard had made his mark in life.

People would assume that, as Stephen was a famous novelist, with many copies of his books sold worldwide, he was wealthy, and he should be wealthy. But Stephen had to have the most expensive cars and holidays, the smartest clothes, and his extravagant lifestyle swallowed up his income rapidly.

"I would be happy to help out. Of course we must honour Chloe's memory."

"Thank you so much, you are a star. I will pay you back with interest!"

Richard ignored those words. "If you want any help arranging it all, I am happy to help."

"Fantastic, I thought I would include Anna as well. She thought a lot of Chloe."

"Great stuff. She will know what Chloe's favourite songs were, and other personal details that we never got to find out."

Stephen suddenly realised how true that was. In a year of marriage, they had never discussed Chloe's favourite music. He blamed himself, as he had always been in his study writing, but it was too late to change that now, because Chloe was gone.

Zoe walked into the doctor's surgery with a certain amount of trepidation. She knew that Dr Kelly was a kindly man who did not judge anybody, but inside her was the feeling of guilt that she had lost control of her life, and was letting her husband and children down. With all her years of training as a nurse, how had this happened?

"Good morning, Zoe. Do come and sit down."

"Thank you, doctor."

"I have invited you to come here today and speak to me before anything else happens. I am just your family doctor, and I do not deal with mental health issues, but I would like you to explain to me exactly what is going on in your mind."

Zoe had always found him easy to talk to. He was about the same age as her dad, with twinkly blue eyes and a friendly face. He felt like a kind uncle. She poured out all her thoughts to him; her feeling of numbness towards Erica, her feeling of continual weariness, her disappointment with herself for being unable to breastfeed, and the inexplicable bleakness that she felt inside.

After she had finished, Dr Kelly adjusted his glasses and paused before he spoke. Being a father and a family man himself, with a job that often took him out at unusual hours, he could understand how she felt. Her husband was a high profile detective with a very important job. His own wife had struggled in the past, so he wanted to reassure Zoe she was not alone.

"Zoe, you are a very special person. Without your support, it would be very hard for Alan to achieve the success that he has in his job."

"I hadn't thought of it that way. Only that I was letting him down."

"Have you told Alan how you feel?"

"A little bit, but I don't want to distract him from the case."

"It's very important that you tell him. I can offer you counselling with a specialist if you want. I can also offer you medication, if it will help, but I promise you that feeling of numbness towards Erica will go."

"How do you know?" she whispered bemused.

"Because it happened to my wife, and her closeness to our daughter now is so tight."

"I know I am a lucky woman. Two beautiful healthy children, a caring husband and no money worries. This is why I just don't understand what is wrong with me."

"Nobody is safe from postnatal depression. It doesn't pick and choose who it will affect. But the most important thing is to recognise that this is only a temporary phase, and you will get better. Don't try and hide it from your husband, he needs to know. Don't shut him out."

"I will tell him. I am rubbish at keeping secrets anyway. I don't want to take any pills if I don't need to. As for counselling, I don't really have any issues to discuss. I believe you when you say I will get better, so I guess my fate is in my own hands."

"It is, but don't be too hard on yourself. Take every bit of support and help that is offered to you, and don't forget your body needs time to recover from the birth. You will know when you feel better; that is when you find you want to take up the reins again, and be in charge."

"Thank you so much, Dr Kelly."

Zoe left the surgery feeling so much better. Maybe she wasn't a failure if it had happened to his wife, as she had worked alongside him for years as a receptionist and secretary, and Zoe had always thought how efficient she was.

When she got home, she took Dr Kelly's advice. After making sure that Monique had given Adam his lunch, she picked up Erica and fed her. The baby fed well from the bottle, and Zoe was pleased at how easily she was able to get her wind up. Then she settled her back into her cot to sleep it off.

"Can you take Adam out for a walk this afternoon, please, Monique? I am going to take a rest."

Monique nodded, but her expression was not particularly happy. "Is there something wrong?"

"I was going to feed Erica. I usually do."

Zoe was mystified. What was going on here? The nanny was trying to take over her baby. But then she realised this was her own fault. Her baby was now three weeks old, and this was probably the first time since she had given up trying to breastfeed her, that she had picked her up and fed her. She had made Monique feel it was her responsibility, and that she, Monique, had failed.

"It's OK Monique. I am not used to bottle feeding, and I wanted to give it a try. It went well. Your support is everything to me right now," she said, smiling brightly. The last thing she wanted to do was lose her nanny.

Monique nodded in response, but inside she was not happy. This woman had everything she could possibly want; a doting husband, a nice house and beautiful babies. Her jealousy rose inside her like a deadly poison, ready to destroy everything around it. She had expected her last employer to be like putty in her hands, but he had controlled her. She had put up with it because he scared her. Then she got pregnant, but later she had miscarried.

But this time it was not going to go wrong. She had her sights set on handsome DCI Alan Clarke. What a catch! Already Erica felt like her baby, and as for Adam, he was an absolute delight. They could be their own happy family, and she would never have to go back to the squalid flat in Paris.

Alan was pleased to see Zoe looking more relaxed when he got home from work that evening. There was a delicious aroma coming from the kitchen, which was very welcoming. He wrapped her into his arms, whilst Adam was pulling at his leg trying to distract him, and they both laughed.

"Let me cuddle your lovely mum," he laughed.

"Adam, it is time for your bed," said Monique, scooping him up.

"We'll come and say goodnight in a minute, son," promised Alan, as he watched Monique carrying Adam from the room. He had mixed feelings about having a nanny. There was relief because Zoe was getting the support she needed, but having an au pair had meant the nanny living in, and he liked having his own space with Zoe at the end of the day. Monique had a habit of fixing her sorrowful eyes on him, and he wondered whether she might be a bit lonely away from home and in a foreign country. They had given her the largest spare bedroom with its own en suite and she had a big TV in there, and all sorts of modern amenities. The agreement had been that she was free after six, either to retire there, or go out with friends. But after being at work all day, he valued his evenings with Zoe.

"Do you think she's going out tonight?" he whispered to Zoe after she had left the room.

"I hope so. I want to tell you something," whispered back Zoe, and they both giggled conspiratorially.

Alan waited a few minutes, and then went in to say goodnight to Adam, who was sitting up in his cot, holding a baby book. "OK son, let's read about all the animals," he grinned, knowing this would be an excuse to indulge in making ridiculous animal noises to entertain his son.

Zoe had to smile, her boys were both as bad as each other. So she joined Alan, and they had fun snorting like pigs and barking like dogs, whilst Adam was doing his best to copy them and having fits of laughter.

Her duties for the day now done, Monique went into her bedroom. It was a warm evening, and people were still on the beach. Her bedroom window overlooked the beach and, although it was past six o'clock, the tide was high, and people were swimming in the sea. This was exceptionally warm weather for May, and they were making the most of it.

She put on a pair of white shorts with a light peach tee shirt. Her legs were always permanently tanned, and although she was not beautiful, she knew her legs were her greatest asset. Her slim figure and long legs gave her confidence, and she moved like a cat stalking its prey.

She popped her head round the door of Adam's room. They were obviously having fun in there, and she felt out of it. They clearly did not need her right now.

"I am going to the pier to meet my friend. I have a key," she said.

"Of course, Monique, and thank you for your help today," said Zoe, smiling in a kindly way. But Monique's face remained serious.

After she had gone, they both tucked Adam up and checked on Erica, and then returned to the lounge.

"Do you think she's got a boyfriend?" asked Zoe.

"Probably, she's got her legs out," laughed Alan.

"So you noticed, then?" laughed Zoe, making a mental note to see if she still fitted into her shorts. Alan hadn't seen her legs since last summer.

"Let's not talk about her, though. You said you had something to tell me."

They both sat down together at the table in the garden, which gave a stunning view over the beach and the downs. Alan poured them both some Sangria and included slices of lemon and ice cubes, and they sipped at the cool liquid. Zoe then proceeded to tell him about her visit to the doctor, and what had been discussed. When she had finished, he looked at her with concern.

"Honey, you know we can afford to go private. You only have to say the word."

"I know, Alan, but I think I can fight it without all that. Knowing that it affects other people too makes me feel better, and having you and Monique. I am going to try, anyway."

"Well honey, I know what a strong woman I am married to, but don't struggle alone. We will get through this together."

He got up from his chair and hugged her close. She was the love of his life, and the mother of his children, and he appreciated the way she had always supported him. Now it was his turn.

"How about some Chinese takeaway from that nice place in Beltinge? I believe they deliver, too. I don't want you cooking this evening."

"Sound lovely," murmured Zoe, holding up her glass for him to refill it. She could turn out the gas under the casserole, and it would do for tomorrow.

The pier was still full of activity when Monique reached it. During summer evenings people still wanted to buy ice creams, and the man was still there cooking burgers outside his little wooden hut.

She sat down at one of the tables to wait until Kay arrived, then they could order something together. Kay would have an excuse to be late, as she had travelled in from Broadstairs. But luckily her boss Stephen had allowed her to use his late wife Chloe's car to run around in, as it was just standing parked in the road not being used.

"I am just waiting for my friend," she said to the man, who had looked up when she sat down, and he nodded back. A couple of minutes later, Kay, also dressed in shorts, came onto the pier and walked towards her.

"Hi Monique, just managed to get parked."

Monique smiled at her. Kay had been a lifesaver for her, and a useful friend to have.

"I have not eaten, so am having a burger. How about you?"

Kay's face lit up. It had been a long day. "That sounds nice."

Monique bought coffees for both of them, and they sat there enjoying the evening sun whilst the man cooked them both a burger. "How is it all going then?" asked Kay.

"It's a lovely house, and so are the babies. I would certainly like to live there all the time."

"How are you going to manage that?" said Kay, laughing, but then she realised that Monique was not joking, and she became worried.

"Well, thanks to you, and the great reference you gave about me, I am in. It's been the best three weeks of my life."

"Yes, but you know it's not permanent, just to help out until their mother is better. I know it's sad what happened to you, but they are not your babies, Monique!"

Monique curled her lip in disgust. "Their mother is a spoilt, rich wife. She has two lovely children, but complains she can't bond with her baby! If she had lost her baby like I did, she would know what real depression is!"

"But that is not a reason for you to cause any trouble in their marriage," said Kay. "This man is a high profile figure in the police force, and if anyone found out you had a false reference, you and I would both be in serious trouble."

Monique laughed. "No worries. Just eat your burger; it's ready now."

After they had both eaten, they walked along to the bandstand where some live music was playing. They stopped there for a while and had an ice cream sundae. But although the subject was not mentioned again, Kay became worried. She was beginning to realise that Monique was a bit of a loose cannon. Whatever had she done? She should never have got involved with her.

Later on, when she was in bed at Broadstairs, she tossed and turned. Her own position was safe enough. Chloe was dead, and if anything developed between herself and Stephen, it wouldn't be that surprising, as not only did he have a very young baby to bring up, but also he was a lonely widower. But Monique seemed to have set her sights on destroying a marriage, yet again, and that could expose both of them.

Chapter Thirteen

"Chloe Ward's funeral is going to take place at Thanet Crematorium on 7th June at eleven o'clock, sir, and they have requested our presence there," said Martha.

"OK, can I leave that to you then? We will attend in uniform," said Alan.

"Yes sir," said Martha, clicking her phone off. "Apparently Stephen Ward has pulled out all the stops to make it a big and beautiful occasion to honour such a short life. He has consulted Anna about Chloe's favourite music and poems etc. There will be a coach with white horses to take her to the chapel, and most of Kent has been invited."

"Did he tell you all this?"

"No, Anna did. She has changed her opinion of him, and says he truly misses Chloe, and his next book has been inspired by her short life, because he wants to write about their love story, how they met and fell in love in Crete."

"Well, that all sounds wonderful, I am sure, but that is seeing life through rose coloured glasses. I suppose that is what writers of romantic fiction do. But it's not true to life," said Alan, He could have added that nobody for sure knew who was baby Luke's real father, a gypsy or a writer, but it sounded spiteful and malicious. All he was interested in was finding Chloe's killer, and after initially thinking about Stephen Ward, his attention was now turned towards Vince Mulligan, who in his mind ticked a lot of the boxes as to why he might have killed Chloe. James and his crew had been instructed to bring him in for further questioning, as he was going to be charged for the third time for possession of cannabis, and this time it would be more than just a fine.

Whilst he was waiting for James, he flicked through the papers again. They had discounted the silk scarf as being any sort of evidence, because so many of the witnesses had touched it for one reason or another. He cast his mind back again to Sam Turner, who had been found at the scene by Thanet police. If the boy had done it and panicked, he would have to lie to save his skin. He wasn't stupid, far from it, in fact. And as for his mother, any mother would defend their son, it was human nature, but had Sam fooled his mother into believing him? Out of all the suspects, Alan wished with all his heart that it wasn't Sam. But he knew, if it was, he would have to be punished the same as any other murderer, and being autistic was not an excuse. Could someone who had always been so gentle and timid, suddenly attack and murder someone because they lusted after them? Had he snapped because his advances had failed?

Tests done on the body afterwards had found there to be no signs of rape or any sort of attack, and Chloe had not been carrying any money on her, so nobody had robbed her. Indeed she had died very peacefully, seemingly unaware that someone had tightened her scarf and strangled her. Which brought him back to Vince, he was the only one likely to have given her heroin. It must be Vince, surely?

"You might as well get out now. You promised me no more drugs!"

"But it was only a bit of weed, I promise you, babe!"

Lena O'Mara's eyes flashed, as she used every swear word she could think of in an expletive ridden rant. "You think I am stupid, Vince. I know why you go up there at night to the van. You pick up tarts, drink brandy and ply them with drugs! I am so done with you!"

"But our babes!"

"If you cared about our babes, you would be here with me taking care of them. I know exactly what you are, and this time you went too far, and you killed her. So if you think I am going to allow you anywhere near our babes, you are so wrong!"

"You can't believe that about me!" sobbed Vince. But it made no difference. The caravan door was shut firmly in his face. He turned to see Lena's father glowering at him. He was a big, bulky man, and Vince knew who would come off worse in a fight. He had just the clothes he was wearing, and there was no way he was going to be allowed back in to get anything.

He felt himself being roughly pushed onto the ground, and felt blood dripping from his nose.

"Now get outta here. You brought shame on us all, you murderer!"

Alan's mobile rang, and he picked it up quickly.

"Yes, James."

"We are at the caravan, sir, but Mulligan is not here. He's gone."

"What do you mean gone?"

"His missus threw him out for good now. Her father says they want nothing more to do with him, and he's gone."

"Well you best pull out all the stops to find him. Presumably he has taken the van."

"No sir. He will be on foot, the van belongs to the fair. It's part of the equipment."

"OK James, you might as well come back here. We'll have to think of something else."

Alan cleared down, and Martha saw his face. He was angry. "What's happened, sir?"

"Mulligan has gone missing. His missus has thrown him out, and now he has gone walkabout. We must find him. If he is the murderer, then he is a dangerous man. I've told James to come back here, and then we will have to do a nationwide appeal, and get the public to keep an eye out for him as well."

"If he's from Ireland, he might have relatives there who will hide him."

"I think his family are part of the fair, and they have all disowned him. That speaks volumes, that they think he's capable of murder," said Alan darkly.

James was back within the hour, and Martha contacted the press to sit in on a public appeal for Mulligan to give himself up.

"But nobody must approach him. This man is dangerous!" emphasised Alan.

Another hour passed, and many members of the press had gathered. So, with Martha sitting beside him, Alan first of all appealed to Mulligan to give himself up, promising, if he did, they would go easier on his sentence. Then he appealed to the public, for anyone who saw him to come forward and help them with their enquiries. But he also gave a word of warning that nobody was to approach him, because he was a danger to the public.

Road blocks were set up in certain areas, and ferries were checked in case he was trying to get abroad.

But all this was after Vince had got onto the Irish ferry that left from Dover to Ireland. He was now convinced that he would be charged with Chloe's murder. There was only one person in the world who would believe him if he said he was innocent; his mother. She had been estranged from the rest of the family years ago, and lived quietly in a little cottage not far from the ferry terminal. She had a smallholding there, with chickens and ducks, and she also grew fruit and vegetables. This just about gave her enough of an income to live on since she had split up with his father some fifteen years previously.

When Vince arrived, she was out working in the fields. He was very hungry, so he made himself a pot of tea, and found some bread to eat. He knew it would be a shock seeing her after all these years. She had never approved of him joining the fair, and had never met Lena. But his mother had broken the golden rule within the family, and slept with her husband's brother. He had left her, but she had broken gypsy honour, so the rest of the family disowned her. Vince had not really cared one way or another, but now he had been disowned, so as far as he was concerned, Vince and his mother needed to stick together.

He was sitting at the table eating when his mother came in from the fields, accompanied by her faithful collie Max, who bounded over ready to share his food.

"Begorrah, 'tis my son Vince I see here," she shook her head in disbelief. "What might you be wanting from me this day?"

"Mam, I am on the run. I was just havin' a bit a harmless fun.

They say I killed her but I didn't. Just gave her a bit a weed, and later they found her dead."

Erin Mulligan was forty-six, but with a life spent mainly outside on the land in all weathers, she looked older. Her skin was a little wizened, and her hair had already turned grey. She wore it back from her face, and she had jeans and a faded tee shirt on. For her, survival was more important than glamour.

"No son of mine is a killer," she muttered, her small bird like eyes fixed on him.

"But how can you stay here? It will soon be in our newspapers, and on the news. You mustn't show your face at the shop."

"No mam, I will lay low. I will stay here, and then, when it all calms down, I can maybe change my appearance. Shave my hair off, wear a hat. I dunno, but I'll think of something."

"Shave off your beautiful curls," she said, brokenly, remembering the bonny little boy he had been.

"It's better than being in prison!" said Vince.

After the press conference, the news about Vince's disappearance spread everywhere. It was now on social media, and the staff were kept busy with calls from the public, many purporting to have seen Vince in various different places. This was normal whenever public appeals took place, and now it was the job of the staff to investigate all of them to see if any of the sightings were going to lead to capturing him.

Police had gone to Dover to try and interview the rest of the travellers, but were not successful in getting any information. No matter how angry Lena was with Vince, she remained tight-lipped, as did the rest of the family, as to where he might have fled to.

Despite Martha's earlier comments, Alan and his team were unaware that Vince's mother lived in Ireland, away from the rest of the family. So airports were particularly of interest, and Channel crossings, in case he had fled the country, but it seemed like he had vanished into thin air.

Chapter Fourteen

The day of the funeral was cloudy and grey, which added very much to the sadness of the occasion. It didn't even feel like a summer's day, and it was windy. Stephen had arranged for the coach and white horses to move slowly up Albion Street, and make slow progress to Thanet Crematorium.

The whole day had been carefully planned and Richard had not told anyone that he had footed the bill, so it was assumed that Stephen had paid for it. He had involved Anna in the choice of music. Cold Play was Chloe's favourite group, and because she had shown herself to have a romantic nature, it was not hard to choose a poem that fitted the occasion.

Just as they reached Albion Street the rain started and the wind howled, it was a feeling of great unrest, as though the spirits were angry that Chloe had been taken at such a young age. Anna sat between Stephen and Richard in the limousine. The streets were empty, and it seemed like a ghost town.

Her parents were following behind in their car with other guests, and there would be even more people meeting up with them at the crematorium. Stephen and Richard both looked immaculate in black suits and white dress shirts, set off by shiny shoes. Anna was also wearing black; a mid calf length dress with a pencil skirt, and black stiletto heels. Over the top she was wearing a black hooded raincoat.

She had been impressed by the respectful way that Stephen had treated her, and she found herself warming to him even more as she got to know him better. She felt ashamed that she had jumped to conclusions about him in the past. Richard was also an absolute gentleman. He had impeccable manners, but she couldn't help wondering if he was lonely, as during their conversation Stephen had told her Richard had lost his partner two years ago. They had been living together for ten years, but Ed had committed suicide. She had been shocked to hear this.

When they arrived at Thanet Crematorium, many people were gathered outside. Stephen greeted them all briefly, and Anna saw the tears in his eyes when the coffin was carefully brought out of the coach. Without even thinking about it, she gripped his hand in support. "It's OK, Stephen," she whispered. Then she saw him make a supreme effort, and after nodding at Richard, they both took their places with the other pall-bearers, in order to carry the coffin into the church.

Alan and Martha were standing there, having been invited as well. They were both dressed smartly in uniform, but they tried to make themselves inconspicuous amongst the other mourners. Stephen had felt they should be there. Although Chloe's killer had not yet been apprehended, their presence would be comforting to the other guests. The only person missing was Kay, as it was thought that such a young baby had no need to be at his mother's funeral, and she was at the house taking care of him.

On top of the coffin was a photograph of Chloe, her hair was blowing in the breeze, and the auburn lights in her hair glowed. She was smiling, with one of her hands touching the scarf round her neck. Alan could see just how beautiful she had been, and felt that it was sad that she had worried so much about her birthmark.

The chapel was full of people. Some were connected to Chloe, either school friends, or people who knew her from living in Broadstairs all her life. Then there were others who were fans of Stephen, and curiosity had brought them to help celebrate the short life of his wife.

Alan glanced over at Stephen, at the point when the curtains were slowly drawn around the coffin. He was dabbing his eyes with a tissue, clearly very moved by the whole thing. But it didn't escape his notice that Anna was beside him, comforting him as well. She was certainly getting much closer to him, and to Alan that felt suspicious. He decided he would discuss it with Martha later. The trouble with being a detective is he had to be suspicious of everyone.

Vince Mulligan was, of course, the main suspect. He had behaved guiltily, admitted giving her drugs, and then run away to avoid being brought in for further questioning. He had been gone for two weeks now, and appeared to have vanished off the side of the earth. But just because Vince was the person most likely to have done the deed did not mean the case was closed. Indeed, far from it.

In a lot of murder cases, the culprit had turned out to be a member of the family, and certainly Stephen had benefited greatly from Chloe's death. It was obvious that Anna had also been charmed by him, and totally changed her opinion of him, or had that all been planned? It was all continually going round inside his head, he even had dreams about it at night. So whilst Mulligan remained at large, he just didn't know who was guilty.

The music was playing, and Stephen and Richard, with Anna walking beside them, exited the chapel. They all shook hands politely and thanked the vicar for the lovely service. Then everyone walked round to where the flowers were arranged on the ground. It had now stopped raining, so everyone stopped to take in the display. Although donations to a mental health charity had been requested, there were still a lot of flowers, and they contained heartfelt messages from many, expressing sorrow that Chloe had been taken at such a young age.

The guests were all going back to The Royal Albion Hotel, where the wake was being held, but Alan and Martha had declined Stephen's offer to go there. With the service now over, they felt they had done what had been asked, and it was time to head back to the station.

After two weeks in hiding at his mother's cottage, Vince was beginning to feel much safer. His disappearance no longer dominated the news every night. Instead, on this particular day, it was mentioned that Chloe Ward had now been laid to rest, and her husband and family had arranged a beautiful service of remembrance, particularly poignant because of the moving address that her best friend Anna had given about her.

They were probably still looking for him abroad. It was always assumed that fugitives from the law would go abroad, but Vince felt he had the last laugh there. He was in the most obvious place in the world, where he had been born and lived for many years, and the police didn't even know about it. Up until that day, he had kept a low profile, and any help he gave to his mother, either cutting lettuces or cabbages, or collecting eggs had been done at dusk when no one would recognise him. But Vince was tired of hiding away. He wanted to go to the local pub and enjoy a Guinness, and look up some of his old school friends. But when he suggested it to Erin, she became very angry.

"Don't be so stupid. The local police will be round here as soon as they hear. Do you really want to go back to prison? You, my son, have made your bed, and you must lie on it!"

Vince knew she was right, but he did not like being cooped up. He had joined the funfair because they were continually moving around, and he enjoyed the freedom. He had cut his hair very short, which he hated really, but it did make him look different, and he always wore a cap on his head now, and dark glasses, which he felt totally changed him.

He was missing his children, but doubted whether Lena would ever let him see them again. They would grow up not knowing him, and would believe that their father was a murderer on the run. So on an afternoon when it was raining, and quite cold, he went on the till at the farm shop whilst his mother was out in the sheds gathering eggs that had just been laid. Into the shop came Michael O'Leary, who had been in his class at school.

Michael recognised him straight away, but pretended he knew nothing about Vince being on the run. They chatted about school, and old times, and Vince was really starting to let his guard down. But Michael had never forgotten that Vince had stolen his girlfriend when they were at school and he had never forgiven him. Now was the perfect time to exact revenge.

Michael called into the local police station on his way home, and

96

he gave the duty constable Tom Sullivan all the information that he needed for him to organise a raid on Erin's smallholding.

When Vince heard the screech of brakes as the police car pulled up, he knew exactly what was happening. He ran out of the shop in a blind panic. Where on earth could he go? When he saw them advancing towards him, he ran across the road, failing to notice a white van turning the corner. The driver did not have time to avoid him, he did his best to pull his steering wheel in the opposite direction, but the van continued towards Vince rapidly and he was hit by the wing. The driver watched with horror as Vince's body was tossed up into the air, just like a rag doll, his arms and legs seemed to be everywhere. Then he hit the concrete with a thud, face downwards, with blood trickling from out of his mouth.

e

Chapter Fifteen

"Good evening, sir. I have news about the suspect Vince Mulligan. He was spotted serving in a farm shop, apparently owned by his mother. Of course, he tried to run away. . ."

". . .Not again!" groaned Alan, this was all so frustrating.

"He ran across the road, sir, and got hit by a van."

"Oh no. Is he OK?"

"That is it, sir, we don't know as yet. He is in hospital in a coma, and they have not said if he will recover or not, we just have to wait."

Alan couldn't help thinking that, if he did die, they would never know for sure if Vince had killed Chloe. Running away had made him appear to be guilty, but it might just be that he didn't want to go back inside. Just handling drugs would be enough to convict him of something, but proving he had murdered Chloe would be harder.

"Which hospital is he in, James?"

"Belfast City."

"So he did go to Ireland. How on earth did he get through without being spotted?"

"Who knows, sir, but local police have explained his mother lives there, and apparently he has been hiding at her cottage."

"Well thanks, James. I need to be kept informed about his condition and, if there is any improvement, I will personally go and interview him myself."

"Certainly sir, we all have to hope he does pull through."

Alan clicked off his phone and turned to Martha, who was busy catching up on some paperwork.

"They have tracked down Mulligan. He was staying with his mother in Ireland, so your hunch was right."

"Nevertheless, I can't believe we didn't know about her," said Martha. "Did I hear you say he is in hospital?"

"Nobody from the fair told us anything about any relatives anywhere else. They all stuck together."

He then went on to describe how Vince had been discovered, and how he had run off in a panic.

"Are you convinced he is guilty, sir?" asked Martha.

Alan paused before he spoke. "Let's say he is the most likely of the suspects to have done it. I can't imagine he was too thrilled when Chloe told him he might be Luke's father. Then we know he gave her drugs. It would have only taken a minute to strangle her with that scarf if he had lost his temper with her."

"What will happen if he doesn't pull through?"

"Good point. We never like to leave a murder unsolved, and we can't be sure that the other suspects are innocent, so we are still keeping a watch on them."

"I tell you what I think is strange, sir. After telling us that she thought Chloe was being manipulated by Stephen, suddenly Anna seems to have got very close to Stephen, and now he can do no wrong in her eyes."

"Yes, I have to agree it was quite a turnaround, but I think it was because Stephen and Richard consulted her when planning the funeral service, and also, don't forget, she gave a very moving speech about Chloe."

"True, but also Stephen is a romantic novelist, a very handsome man, with a bucket load of charm, and he is sensitive. Women love a man who is sensitive. Personally I believe she has fallen for him, and would be more than happy to be the next Mrs Ward."

Alan grinned at her. "Sounds like you are hooked on him too."

"Not at all. He's not my type, and he is in his own world of romantic fiction, but I can see how he may have won her over."

"What do you make of Richard Lyon?"

"Not a lot, actually. He is a professional man and he doesn't have

99

a lot to say for himself. He's obviously a good friend to Stephen, but I just don't think he has got the courage to murder anyone. Not only that, what would his motive possibly be?" said Martha.

"Maybe he was feeding her heroin, and she threatened to tell on him," mused Alan. "But he would have to have a reason to do that. After all, if found out, that would be his career ruined, and don't forget we searched the homes of all the suspects and no heroin was found."

"I know, sir. In fact, since I have been in the force, I have become a nasty person, always thinking people are potential murderers."

They both laughed, it always felt good to voice their theories to each other.

"On that note, I think it's time we went home. It's been a long day," said Alan, knowing that if he left now, he could make it home in time to bath Adam.

Monique wondered if Alan was on his way home yet. She knew he would try and get in before she finished, and then he would want to bath Adam. In her fantasy world, she could see her future with Alan and the two babies. Adam was such a delightful little boy, and baby Erica was six weeks old, she was beginning to smile and look around herself. Every time she picked her up, she felt happiness and pain in equal measure, because, in her mind, Erica was the replacement for that heartbreaking miscarriage she had suffered last year.

The doctor had told her that, when she felt ready, she would be able to conceive again, but it wasn't that easy. Dan had not even comforted her, and told her quite flatly he was never going to leave his wife. At that moment of extreme anguish, her hatred and jealousy rose, she had not been able to control it, one push at the top of the stairs and Melissa had tumbled.

Dan had actually been the reason she had not been arrested for attempted murder. Luckily Melissa had recovered, and he had done everything to prevent Melissa finding out about their affair. They insisted her fall was an accident, but of course Monique had to go. Then she had found herself homeless in England, resigned to having to return to that squalid flat in the back streets of Paris. The agency had not wanted to keep her on their books, but that is when she met Kay. They both needed a job, so why not provide each other with really good references. So Kay was now installed with Stephen Ward, and Monique was with Alan and Zoe.

But Zoe was a real thorn in the flesh. She just didn't know how lucky she was, married to a powerful and very charismatic man, two beautiful healthy children, and loads of money. Monique didn't think she deserved any of it, and as each day passed, she was getting closer and closer to the children. Alan was harder to get close to because he always seemed to have work on his mind; that is when he wasn't fussing over Zoe. Monique could feel her jealousy rising when she saw him with Zoe. She was biding her time, but she knew she would find a way to get rid of Zoe, and then they could all live happily ever after.

Kay was beginning to realise she had made a huge mistake by befriending Monique. They had both belonged to the same nanny agency, and when she realised the agency couldn't help her because she didn't have the necessary qualifications, she had been in despair. Monique had been working for a family at the time, but had offered to give her a fake set of references; so good, that it was unlikely her employer would check to see if she was fully qualified.

So when Stephen has advertised for a daily nanny to take care of his young son, and support his wife in her early days of motherhood, she went for the interview armed with her glowing references. Then she found out that it was the famous writer Stephen Ward, and she felt so proud that she was working there. But gradually everything had changed.

First of all, there were Chloe's instability and mood changes. It seemed to cast a feeling of gloom over the house. Stephen's way of coping with it was to shut himself in his study and write, leaving her to try and cope with Chloe.

Then, six weeks ago, Monique had needed a reference. But Kay had not realised that it was to work for a member of the police force until after Monique had got the job. She had also believed that

Monique had lost her other job because she had been pregnant and her boss didn't want to leave his wife. She felt even more sorry for Monique when she was told that she had miscarried, and decided Monique needed a second chance.

But during recent meetings with Monique, she realised she was unbalanced. She had pushed one woman down the stairs to get what she wanted, and was now threatening to do the same to another one.

As if that wasn't enough, Chloe had now been murdered, and in a weak moment, because she felt so sorry for Stephen who was totally devastated, she had offered to move in. But, upon reflection, that had not been a good move. The police had been frequent visitors to the house, asking all sorts of questions, and even turning it upside down to check for drugs. How long would it be before Alan Clarke found out that both she and Monique had false references? Not only that, this was no longer a family home, and as much as she loved baby Luke, she didn't feel safe any more. She had given up her flat in Ramsgate to move in here, and was now homeless, and how could she be sure that whoever had carried out the murder might not strike again?

Kay had left home five years ago at the age of eighteen, mainly because she didn't see eye to eye with her parents, but she had kept in touch. She felt she was older and wiser now at twenty-three, so she was going to swallow her pride and move back home for a bit.

Since Anna had started fawning all over Stephen, she had felt superfluous. She told herself they could certainly manage without her, and once she left here and returned home back north in Yorkshire, she would not leave a forwarding address. So if Monique did do something stupid, they would not be able to trace her. The last time she met Monique, she had said nothing about going, but had checked with her parents that she could come home to stay for a while.

Her next move had been a bit more difficult, getting away. She had to leave some of her clothes behind, but she packed a few important things into a small suitcase. Stephen had gone to visit Richard in Ramsgate, as they were going to the club to play tennis, and Anna had offered to have Luke for the afternoon, and introduce him to her parents. Saturday was usually Kay's day off, so she thought she was doing a favour for Stephen, and this made Kay smile, because Anna was actually doing the biggest favour ever for Kay, by making it possible for her to escape this house and go back to the safety of her home.

She gave one last look around her before she left. The only person she would miss was baby Luke. This seemed to be a house full of secrets, but now that Chloe was gone, she was going too, back home where she knew she would be safe.

Chapter Sixteen

"Richard, what am I going to do? Kay has run out on me."

Richard answered him cautiously. Over the years they had been friends, he was well aware of Stephen's fatal charm with women, so nothing would surprise him.

"What happened to make her do this?"

"I have no idea, but I can't manage Luke on my own. It's not just that, I know the police are suspicious of me already with losing Chloe, then suddenly our nanny disappears without a trace."

Richard wrinkled his brow and thought about it. It was true, once the police got wind of Kay's disappearance they would be round to the house again, asking so many awkward questions.

"Have you tried her mobile?"

"Yes, it just goes into voice mail."

"Would you like me to pop round to her flat in Ramsgate and see if I can talk to her?"

"Oh, Richard, would you? We need to find out what's going on."

"In the meantime, you need to get onto the agency and find another nanny."

"Anna has offered to hold the fort until I do, and she is very good with Luke."

Richard knew what was happening here. He had seen it happen before. Anna was willing to do anything to help Stephen because she had her own ulterior motive, it was obvious.

"Just a word of warning about that. You do realise that Anna wants you, to put a finer point on it, to be a couple."

Stephen grimaced at the end of the telephone. "Anna and I have a connection because we both loved Chloe, but apart from that, I have no interest in her."

"Well I suggest you get another nanny as quickly as you can, because if she realises that, she might suddenly not be available. Stephen, women are funny creatures, 'hell hath no fury', is certainly true, you must have learned that by now."

Stephen made no comment to that remark. It was an outside hope that Kay would be at that flat in Ramsgate, because he remembered her telling him she had left, and forfeited her rent for the last month because she had not given proper notice. He had been grateful that someone was there at night in case Luke woke up. He had not handled his son very much as Chloe and Kay had done it between them. But now, suddenly, neither of them were there.

Richard was thinking much the same thing as he drove down the hill towards the outskirts of Ramsgate, where Kay had lived. After ringing the bell several times, he could see she was no longer there. He was due to go back to Harley Street tomorrow. He had bookings to fulfil but, in the meantime, he had to support Stephen.

When he arrived back at Stone Road, Anna had taken charge of Luke and they were out for a walk, which meant he could speak freely to Stephen.

"I have contacted the agency, and they promised to find me someone quickly," explained Stephen.

"OK, that is good, but I am afraid she has gone. Didn't she come from somewhere in Yorkshire?"

"Yes, but I don't have the address. Honestly, I don't want her to come back."

"My advice, Stephen, is to go to the police yourself and report her missing. She has not left a note explaining anything. If you know you have done nothing to upset her, then I think it might be connected to Anna. If you report her missing, and let them find her, then you are off the hook. If they find her alive and well, which they will, they can see that you have done nothing to her. She's just an unreliable nanny, who has let you down."

That made perfect sense to Stephen. What would he do without the common sense of Richard? He really didn't know.

Monique was in a bad mood. She had lost her one and only friend. Kay had not turned up to meet her yesterday, nor offered any sort of explanation. She had tried to ring her phone, but it must be turned off. She didn't think she ought to go over to Broadstairs to the house, they might have found out about their forging of references. She knew she had been fighting fire with fire by taking a position in the house of a policeman, but that was all part of the fun of it. But what annoyed her was that she didn't know what was going on.

She spotted Zoe's keys on the table. Zoe was looking for them in the kitchen, as she had a doctor's appointment in a few minutes. Monique had been told that she would have to walk Adam to play school. It wasn't that far, about half a mile along the road through Beltinge towards Hillborough, but Monique was peeved, they had told her she would have use of the car for Adam. In a moment of spite she hid them. Let Zoe keep looking, she didn't care.

"Have you seen the car keys, Monique? I will be late if I have to walk."

"No," lied Monique. She didn't care if Zoe was late. Anything she could do to press her buttons gave her a sense of malicious pleasure.

"Oh well, I will just have to be late," moaned Zoe. She rushed out of the door. If she didn't get there in time, she might lose her appointment. She had always been a stickler for being on time, so being late stressed her out, but as she walked briskly along the road, she dialled the number of the doctor's surgery. She would not be beaten.

When she got through to the receptionist, she explained that she was on the way, but on foot, so would be a little late. The receptionist assured her that she didn't need to worry, the doctor was running late anyway, so Zoe moderated her pace.

Her appointment was for her six week check up. She was feeling a bit better. Her stomach was shrinking now, but she wasn't back to her normal size yet. She was also thicker around her hips, but now was the time to start doing exercises. It didn't worry her, and Alan didn't even notice, but she always wanted to look her best for him.

She sat down on a chair after checking in. Other people were reading magazines, but Zoe was still puzzled about where her car keys could be. She vowed to take another look when she got home. She was getting so absent-minded lately. Usually they were hanging on a hook near to the door, but not today.

Just at that moment, her name flashed up.

ZOE CLARKE TO SEE DR KELLY, ROOM 3.

She got up and walked along the corridor to room three. The door was closed, so she knocked politely, and the voice of Dr Kelly asked her to come in.

"Good morning, doctor," she smiled as she sat down.

Dr Kelly looked towards her, noting she looked a little flushed today but, apart from that, she seemed quite well. He shuffled his papers.

"So you are here for your post natal examination today. How are you feeling?"

"I am better, doctor. Physically I do not feel so tired, but lately my memory seems to be playing me up. I lost my keys this morning, and was nearly late."

He smiled kindly at her. As busy as he was, he had all the time in the world to listen to her. Zoe did a great job at the hospital, he knew that. She cared about other people more than herself, and she was a great mother. In fact, together with her husband Alan, they both worked conscientiously to make life better for others. So if she was suffering from depression, he would make sure she got all the help she needed. Sometimes depression caused memory loss.

"Well, Zoe, if I counted the number of times I lost my keys, I would lose count. Most of us do that, but I am afraid that just after pregnancy your hormones will play tricks on you, and the memory often suffers."

"It's happening to my mother as well at the moment. She is going through her menopause."

"I expect you are thinking that is the joy of being a woman, but it's not all bad. If you get up on the couch, I will check that everything has healed up as it should."

107

Zoe felt better for telling him. Right now her mind seemed to magnify every mistake that she made, but the reassurance that it also happened to others made her feel better.

After her examination, Dr Kelly assured her that she was doing very well. Her uterus was now back to normal, and the results of a recent blood test had shown that she was not anaemic. This made Zoe feel much better. Her health was very important to her. Having worked in the hospital amongst people with so many difficulties and health problems had made her realise how lucky she was, and never to take it for granted.

"Thank you, doctor. That is good news," she smiled.

"Don't forget, if you ever need us, we are here for you," he reminded her.

"Thank you so much."

When she got outside the surgery, it was such a beautiful day, she walked along the seaside path towards the house. The sea looked so blue today, and the warmth of the sun beamed down upon her. She passed dog walkers. It was a popular spot to walk dogs, as it was away from the road, and parts of the downs overlooking the sea had a maze of little paths for a dog to explore.

By the time she arrived back home, Monique was back from dropping Adam at playschool, and was now feeding Erica. She was smiling and talking softly to the little girl, but Zoe couldn't help noticing how she changed when Zoe came in. She pursed her lips, and avoided talking to Zoe. It seemed that Monique didn't like her very much, but, Zoe reminded herself, Monique was here for her babies, and she loved both of them. That was all that mattered.

Stephen walked into the police station with a determined step. James Martin was talking to the duty constable at the front desk, and he recognised Stephen immediately. He definitely looked like a man on a mission.

"Good morning, Mr Ward, what can we do for you?" he asked, politely.

"Good morning. Is DCI Clarke around? I need to talk to him."

"He is, but right now he's on the telephone. Can I help at all?"

"You certainly can. My nanny has vanished. She left us yesterday without any warning, and I have no idea where she is."

James stiffened with surprise. His first reaction was to think there might have been some sort of argument. But Kay was a young woman, so if she had vanished without trace, they must be concerned about whether she was safe.

"Just wait here a moment, and I will see if DCI Clarke is free."

He left Stephen sitting near to the reception area whilst he went to Alan's office. He had left Alan speaking to the police authorities in Belfast about Vince Mulligan, but when he entered the office Alan was no longer on the phone, he was in a deep discussion with Martha.

"Sorry to interrupt, sir, but Stephen Ward is outside. He has come in to report his nanny missing. Apparently she has vanished without any explanation, and he has no idea where she has gone. "

"Really. There is certainly a lot more going on at that house than we know about," Alan said, thoughtfully. "But I am just trying to persuade Martha here to take a trip to Belfast with me, because Vince Mulligan has woken up and is expected to make a full recovery, so we need to get over to the hospital and interview him."

"Can't you do a zoom interview, sir?" asked James, trying to be helpful.

"Not really, James. The hospital are not keen, and I think I need to be sitting right in front of him to try and get the truth out of him."

"So if you still think it's him, then I think I best go with you, sir," said Martha. If she had a choice between the sunny south east of England or rainy Ireland, she knew which she wanted, but she also wanted to catch and convict the killer of Chloe.

Alan steered his mind away from Mulligan, he knew Martha wouldn't let him down. But it was interesting that the nanny had left. What could be going on there now?

"James, I am going to leave this interview with Stephen Ward to you. I know you will do a good job, you always do. You must record it, of course, so I can take a look at it when we get back. In the meantime, Martha, can you book us return tickets to Belfast today? If we get going now, we might even get a flight back home this evening."

James glowed with pride. It was nice that his boss was so complimentary about him.

"Yes, I can do that, sir, and will have Natalie with me to make sure everything is recorded."

"Good man," said Alan, then glanced over at Martha who was busy on the phone. She nodded at him whilst speaking; it looked like it was all going to work out.

After she had come off the phone, she confirmed that boarding passes would be ready for them, but they needed to go.

"OK, thanks. I just need to let Zoe know in case we take longer than we expect."

He got through to Zoe, and explained about the trip to Ireland, saying it was urgent but he hoped to be back later that evening. Zoe knew about Vince Mulligan being in hospital because it had been all over the press when he had the accident. She also knew how important it was for Alan to interview him, so she injected enthusiasm into her voice at the other end of the phone.

"I understand, Alan, it's fine. I just got back from my six week examination and the doctor says I am doing well."

Alan then remembered, she had told him about the appointment but he had forgotten. There were so many things on his mind. He mentally chided himself. He honestly did not deserve lovely Zoe.

"Honey, that is great news. I will be back just as soon as I can." He turned away, so Martha and James could not hear him, and whispered, "I love you!"

"I love you, too," whispered Zoe back, then she giggled to herself, as Monique was sitting there with a deadpan face. Wasn't she just the world's worst misery?

Chapter Seventeen

"He's awake now, and hopefully will make a recovery. Are you coming to see him?"

Lena hesitated before she answered Sister Bright. The past month had made her regret her angry reaction to Vince's misdemeanours. At the time her love had temporarily turned to hate, it had been good riddance to bad rubbish. She wasn't surprised that he had gone to his mother, as she was probably the only person in the family who would put up with him. But when she heard about his accident, she was filled with horror that he might die. She had always known that Vince was a womaniser, a liar, and he smoked weed. He was a rogue, but he was her rogue, the father of her children, and life was nothing without him. No matter how bad he was, she still didn't believe he was capable of murder, and nobody knew him as well as she did.

"Yes, I would like to visit. I have to travel from England. First I have to find someone to look after my babes, but I will somehow. Can you please tell him Lena is coming soon."

"I certainly will," replied Sister bright. "You will be his first visitor."

Lena clicked off her phone to end the call. She had some cash put away in the caravan which would pay for her air ticket, and she would have to find somewhere to stay. She had never done anything like this on her own before. Living within the gypsy community gave her a certain amount of protection. But the hardest thing was going to be persuading her mother to look after the babes whilst she went to Belfast. She knew her mother thought he was no good, and would not want her to take him back, but then her dad had left them years ago, so her mother had a very poor opinion of men.

She went to see her mother next. Maybe seeing her grandchildren, which she adored, might soften up her tough mother. She knocked on the door, and when Rose opened it, she made sure her arms were full of the two little ones, and they wasted no time in clambering over their granny.

"Ma, I just bin talking to the nursing sister. Vince is out of the coma, and she asked if I was visiting him."

"Did she now? Don't tell me you want that no good back."

"Well Ma, he's ma kids' dad. I don't want 'em to grow up without him."

"Like you did, you mean?"

Lena put her arms around her mother's shoulders, and encircled her children into the hug too.

"I never wanted him to die. He's not a murderer, and the kids and I need him," she said, with a touch of defiance in her tone.

Rose knew it was useless trying to stop her. Lena had always done exactly as she wanted, and no matter how much he had hurt her, she still loved that man. Rose didn't think he was a murderer either. He was many things, but he didn't have the guts to do anything like that.

"So you want to leave the babes with me whilst you go to Ireland then?"

"I do, Mam. I have some cash to buy a plane ticket."

"Cash is no good, girl. You need to go and see Theo, he will do it online with a card. You can give him the cash."

"OK Mam, can you just let him know I am coming over. He won't try and stop me, will he?" she asked, feeling uncertain.

"Nobody will stop you, it's your life. Just leave the bairns with me," said her mother, and Lena rewarded her with a grateful hug.

*　　*　　*　　*

Alan and Martha stepped out of the taxi, entered through the doors of the hospital and then approached the reception area. It was now two o'clock, and they were booked on a six o'clock plane back in the evening. Neither of them had wanted to stay overnight. No matter how tiring this short trip would be, they both wanted to get back home to their own beds later.

The receptionist pointed them in the direction of the side room where Vince was, which was at the end of a long corridor. When they arrived outside, the door was closed, but after looking through a glass panel, Alan saw Vince propped up in bed, with pillows behind him. His face looked pale, and his eyes were closed. There was a nurse standing outside the door, who pointed out Sister Bright to Alan. She was a middle-aged woman with brown hair clipped back at the sides. She was stocky and short, but she had a determined manner about her which forbade anyone to think of disagreeing with her.

"DCI Clarke?" she enquired, holding out her hand briefly to shake his.

"Yes, and my partner Martha," smiled Alan. "We have come to interview Mr Mulligan."

"He's still quite sleepy, so I will come back when I feel he's had enough," she said briskly, whilst opening the door to let them enter the room.

Alan was expecting this. He nodded politely. The figure in the bed stirred and opened his eyes.

"Vince, DCI Clarke is here to speak to you, and also Lena should be here in about an hour."

Alan's ears pricked up at this news, maybe they could interview her, too. She had not been helpful when they had met her just after Mulligan had disappeared, but she had just found out he had been unfaithful to her. She had told Alan that she had thrown Vince out and wanted nothing more to do with him, but it was amazing how a brush with death could instantly change a situation.

Vince did not look happy to see him, and Alan knew he had to use a little compassion whilst interviewing him. He had been very ill, and lucky to survive, but he was also a key witness in the investigation. Bullying had never been his style, especially when there was no certainty that this was the culprit.

"Good morning, Vince. It's nice to see you are feeling a little better, although we appreciate you have had a rough time," he remarked, pleasantly.

This took the wind right out of Vince's sails, as he had expected threats of an arrest as soon as he was better, and the thought of returning to prison was not one he wanted to think about.

"I was nearly a gonner," he muttered.

"And I hear your partner Lena is also on her way to see you. She must have been very worried," Alan reminded him.

"Dunno why, she slung me out."

"Maybe if you tell us the truth, and her as well, she might have a change of heart," said Martha gently. "Anger fades after a while, you know, and I expect your children are missing you."

Alan took his cue from that. The female perspective always helped in an emotional situation.

"Vince, we have travelled over from England to interview you, and we won't keep you any longer than we have to, because everyone wants you to get well again. Martha is going to record our conversation, but I just want a quick run through what happened that evening with Chloe again, and also I would like to know where you got your weed from."

Vince spoke wearily. It seemed there was no escape from them, so he might as well get it over with. "Like I said, I saw her that night. She was agitated. She told me the child might be mine, and I said we couldn't do much about it now, she had a husband and I had Lena. I did give her a puff a ma fag to calm her down. It worked, so I left her sitting there cos I had to get back."

"Yes, OK. So when you left her she was calmer?"

"Yes. The weed I get from a traveller. He comes and goes. I ask no questions, don't even know his name. But I am done with it now. It's caused me nuffin but trouble, ma girl has dumped me."

Alan wasn't sure he believed that. It was an easy get out to say he was not going to take it any more. But it was clear this man needed time to recover. Apparently he had to learn to walk again, so would not be going back to work for quite a while. Before the accident, he had planned to bring him in and charge him for possession of cannabis, and hold him for a while whilst they tried to find more evidence, but now he wasn't sure.

114

"Well Vince, this is your lucky day. But you only get one lucky day," he said sternly. "You are not going to be charged for the cannabis found in your van on this occasion, but if we find any more, then we will come down hard on you!"

Vince visibly brightened. "Ya know, since I bin in here I missed my family so much. I'm gonna make them proud of me when I get outta here. No more weed!"

Just at that moment, Sister Bright bustled back in. "That's enough for now. Vince needs to rest."

Alan and Martha found themselves outside the door. The interview had been much shorter than they had expected, but glancing through the glass panel, they could see that Sister Bright had settled Vince down for a rest.

She came out and shut the door. "He gets tired easily because of the head injury," she explained.

"Of course," said Alan with sympathy. "I was wondering if you would let us have five minutes with Lena when she arrives?"

"Maybe best if you speak to her before she goes in to see him."

"You are very kind," said Alan in his most charming manner. Martha smiled to herself. It always worked, Alan got away with far more than most people because he never intimidated anyone.

"If you want to go and get some tea or coffee, maybe even something to eat, the snack bar is just along the corridor," said Sister Bright, pointing to her right.

"Many thanks," said Alan, and they headed in the direction she had pointed.

Neither of them were hungry, having grabbed a snack at the airport whilst they were waiting for their taxi, but a cup of coffee was always welcome. They sat down at a table by the window, which looked out onto a series of other buildings.

"You were easy on him," laughed Martha. "Is he no longer a suspect?"

"The poor blighter did nearly die, and he is going to need several months to get back to normal. He doesn't need me turning up issuing threats." Martha smiled. This is why she liked working with Alan. Not only was he an astute policeman, he was also a very fair minded one.

"But he's not off the hook yet. Let's keep an eye out for him. But in the meantime, lots seem to be going on at Stone Road. It will be interesting to find out what James learns when he interviews Stephen Ward."

"Yes, we have to wonder if the nanny is safe, and where she has gone."

They sat there chatting over their coffee, and after about half an hour, a message came onto Alan's mobile. It was Sister Bright, she had taken his number, and she confirmed that Lena had arrived, and was prepared to wait and see them before she went in to visit Vince.

They walked along the corridor until they reached the waiting area. Lena was the only person sitting there. She was a tall young woman with curly blonde hair, and she had big hooped golden earrings dangling from her ears. Her face looked a bit anxious when she spotted them. Alan did his best to put her at ease.

"Hi again, Lena, we are pleased to see that Vince is recovering."

Her face relaxed a little. "Yes, Sister Bright says it might take a while, but he can come back soon, and I will take care of him."

"I am glad to hear that," said Alan.

"We do look after our own, and I know he's done some bad stuff, but my Vince would never kill anyone. He ain't got that sort of aggression in him. He even rescues mice from out of the cat's mouth and saves them."

Alan smiled at the comparison, but he was beginning to believe her. "Just one question, Lena. On that night of 24th May, where were you whilst Vince was out?"

"Looking after me bairns, a course," she said emphatically.

"Have you any idea what time he came back?"

"No, I was in my bed. It's tiring work with only a year between them in age."

"Yes, of course, thank you so much for your time. That is all we wanted to know, and let's hope Vince will continue to improve," said Alan politely. Turning to Martha, he suggested they phone for a taxi to get back to the airport. Martha was soon on the case, so they sat in reception waiting for it to come.

Lena took a deep breath before she went in to see Vince. Thank goodness nobody knew she had left the bairns just for a few minutes whilst she went to check up on Vince that night. She knew for sure he had not killed Chloe, but her anger at seeing Chloe hanging about up there, and knowing she was the fancy bit he had been carrying on with, knew no bounds. But that secret was inside her, nobody else, not even Vince knew about that.

Chapter Eighteen

"Thank you for coming round, Constable Martin. Kay is a young woman, and it is out of character for her not to be here, so I thought it best to report her disappearance to you," said Stephen.

"Yes, you did the right thing."

As James spoke, he was hoping that another body would not be found. The last thing they wanted were any more murders. One was bad enough. It was strange that this house seemed to be the centre of such a lot of strange events.

Natalie was busy making notes to be passed on to Alan. She left all the questioning to James.

"When did you actually realise she was missing?"

"Yesterday afternoon, after Anna brought Luke back. Anna offered to look after him, as I wanted to play tennis, and Saturday is usually Kay's day off."

"Was there an upset or argument before she went?"

"Not at all. Kay has always done her job well, and we had no complaints."

"Does Anna also get on OK with her?"

"I have never seen any friction between them."

"I presume you have been round to her flat to check if she is there."

"Richard, my friend did, but she no longer lives there, it's empty."

"Do you know anything about her family, and where they live?"

"Kay lives somewhere in Yorkshire, but I don't know her address."

James took a deep breath. Yorkshire was a big county, but they really had to know that this girl was not in any danger. "In that case, all we can do is contact local police in that area, and ask if they can keep an eye out for her."

"The nanny agency might have her previous address," said Stephen.

"Yes, and so might her landlord," agreed James. "We can look in to that. If all her belongings are gone, it does sound as if she left voluntarily. But because it was so sudden, we need to find her so she can explain why."

"Luckily Anna is helping out at the moment, but I do need another nanny, she has her own job."

"What is her job?" asked James.

"She is a trainee accountant, and works mainly from home. But it's not ideal, after caring for a young baby all day, to have to do it in the evening."

"Very true," agreed James. "Well, thank you for your time, Mr Ward. As soon as we locate her, we will let you know."

"Thank you so much," said Stephen, showing them to the door.

"Well," said Natalie, whilst they were driving back to Canterbury, "it might be hard to find a nanny to work in a house where the mother was murdered; it won't feel like home."

"Yes. You have a point there," agreed James. "I can't help feeling sorry for Stephen Ward. He seems to be utterly lost"

Alan arrived home after ten o'clock. He had dropped Martha off at her flat after picking his car up from the police station. He didn't expect Zoe to still be up, but when he entered the house, she was curled up on the sofa asleep. He put his arms around her gently, so she did not wake up with a start, and she sleepily opened her eyes.

"Honey, you should be tucked up in bed, not waiting up for me," he said, tenderly.

"Oh, I had a bath, and thought I would wait up. Erica might wake up soon for another feed."

"What about Monique. Can't she do it?"

"It's a bit late now, she has probably gone to bed. I heard her having a shower earlier."

Zoe was right about Erica, snuffling noises could be heard coming from the baby alarm, which meant she was waking up for a feed. As tired as he felt, Alan did not want to go to bed without Zoe, so he went into the bedroom and picked up his tiny daughter. Zoe had gone to the fridge, and she came back into the room with the bottle.

"Let's go to bed, and if I may, I would love to feed her," said Alan, holding the warm little baby close to him. Her cry was getting louder now. She was hungry, so he walked through to their bedroom, where her cot was right next to the bed.

Zoe followed after him, holding the bottle. They both got into bed, and she made the pillows behind Alan more comfortable, so he could feed Erica, and lean back against them. Then she brought a clean nappy over, and baby wipes, before getting into bed beside him. Erica fed very sleepily, and Alan held her up to wind her afterwards. She obliged him with a loud burp, and then promptly went back to sleep. He felt inside her nappy, but she felt dry.

"She isn't wet, honey. Don't think I should change her, it will only wake her up."

There was no response, and when he looked over he could see Zoe had fallen back to sleep. He was so glad he had taken charge of feeding Erica. Zoe had looked so tired, and she obviously was to have fallen back to sleep again. He had ignored his own tiredness to give her support, and it felt good that, even after being out of the house for hours, he was still here when she needed him.

He placed Erica back in her cot as she was now sleeping soundly, then got back into bed and cuddled into Zoe's back. "Goodnight honey, I love you," he murmured, and then within a couple of minutes, he, too, was asleep.

James knocked on the door of Alan's office, and a voice bade him to come in.

"Good morning, sir. I hope you had a productive day in Ireland yesterday."

Alan smiled. "Not really, other than thinking I might be wasting time on Vince Mulligan, and he might not be the culprit."

"Well, when we interviewed Stephen Ward, he said he had no idea where Kay had gone. Her flat was empty, and all her belongings have gone, so it looks like she left of her own choice."

"Well then, there must have been some sort of falling out, either with Stephen, or Anna, surely?"

"Stephen spoke highly of her capabilities, and said he was not aware of any friction. He also said that when we find her, he does not want her back as she has destroyed his trust."

"I can understand that, but if we don't know where she has gone, it will be hard to find her."

James cleared his throat. "I was just coming onto that, sir. When I contacted the nanny agency, they confirmed they are trying to find a new nanny, but more importantly, they also confirmed that Kay was not on their books, they did not supply her to Stephen Ward."

Alan stiffened with surprise. "So how did she get the job, then?"

"Apparently the agency did have Kay's details. She tried to register with them, but she didn't have the necessary qualifications, so they said they regretfully had to reject her, and the address they had for her was the Ramsgate one. We went back to see Stephen again. He was very vague about it. He said Chloe had interviewed and accepted Kay, and she had produced very creditable references."

"Right, so she probably found her online," mused Alan, but none of this helps us to find the address in Yorkshire where her parents live. She is most likely to have gone there."

"I do have her address, sir," said James. "Natalie and I managed to speak to her previous landlord. He wasn't too keen until I showed him my pass, and explained it was to help us in a murder enquiry." He passed a piece of paper to Alan, who scanned it quickly. It was in Moortown, Leeds.

"Wow James, you did it. You got the address, you have done well!"

"Thank you, sir."

Alan turned towards Martha, who up until then had been listening intently to the conversation.

f

"It's a bit late to set out today, but guess where we are going tomorrow morning?"

"Oh sir, I have a day off tomorrow. It's my birthday."

"Oh yes, sorry, I had forgotten that!" he exclaimed. "You have a great day. I can manage."

He made a mental note to pop out later and get her a birthday card and a box of chocolates. He could give them to her before he went home.

"I would be happy to come with you, sir, if you want company. I have nothing special on," interjected James. He had actually enjoyed interviewing Stephen. He didn't think the man had killed his wife, but this nanny sounded very dodgy, especially as she had not come from an agency.

Alan thought about it. It would be nice to have a travelling companion. He had already decided he would take the car, as he didn't want to mess about travelling up to London by train.

"James, that would be great. It's quite a long journey, so we will have to leave early in the morning. We might even have to stay overnight."

"Whatever you want to do is fine by me, sir, I will bring an overnight bag just in case."

"OK, sounds good. Martha will sort out the paperwork this afternoon, and I will pick you up at seven o'clock."

James was looking forward to spending the day with him. He had always looked up to Alan Clarke, and aspired to be a DCI himself one day. It would be interesting to interview Kay's parents, and hopefully she would be there too, and able to explain herself, and why she had left so abruptly without telling anyone.

Alan decided that as he was going off for another day, and possibly staying overnight, he would spoil Zoe tonight. He would go home a bit earlier tonight, and maybe if Monique was going to be around this evening, he could take Zoe out for a nice meal. He rang Zoe whilst Martha was getting their morning coffee.

Zoe was sitting out in the garden, enjoying the morning sun, whilst Monique was taking Adam to playschool. Erica had been fed and changed, and was asleep in her cot upstairs. She picked up her mobile when it rang, smiling when Alan's name flashed up. "Yes darling, what can I do for you?"

"Zoe, my love, how about going out for a meal with your adored husband tonight? If Monique condescends to babysit, of course."

Zoe giggled. Alan always had the ability to amuse her, but she knew him well.

"So, where are you off to tomorrow, then?"

Alan explained that he had to go and interview a witness in Yorkshire. James was going with him, and they might even have to stay overnight.

"Why isn't Martha going with you?" she enquired.

Alan groaned. "I forgot it was her birthday. Have to pop out and get her a card. Which do you think she would prefer, flowers or chocolates?"

Zoe smiled, this was something she could do for him. He had helped out with Erica last night, she had been feeling so tired. "Leave it to me. I will get a present and card, and I will pop in with them this afternoon, then I can also wish her happy birthday."

"That would be amazing. She might smell a rat if I suddenly go off shopping, it's not what I usually do."

"OK, so if I come over about three, does that work?"

"It certainly does, and don't forget to book Monique for tonight. I will be home early."

Zoe cleared down on her phone, and she heard Monique pulling into the drive. She waited for her to come into the kitchen, and then went to speak to her. She had not told Alan, but she was finding Monique was very surly towards her, and yet with the children and Alan she was always smiling.

It didn't actually bother her. Privately she thought it was amusing, and it made her even more determined to shake off these bouts of depression. She was feeling almost ready to cope with her children without Monique, and she could do without her pouting face and sullen expression, and September was too far away to put up with it until then. It was amazing that having a negative person around her made her feel more positive in herself. She planned to tell Alan soon, when she felt sure of herself. She put on her most ingratiating smile before she spoke.

"Monique, I was wondering if you have any plans this evening? Alan would like to take me out, and he wondered if you could babysit for us? We will, of course, pay you extra, as you don't normally work in the evening."

Monique felt anger and jealousy coursing away inside; her plan didn't seem to be working. She had tried to make Zoe more depressed by being unfriendly towards her, she had hidden her keys and her phone to stress her out, but Zoe somehow managed to cope with it, and was overjoyed when she found them again. As for Alan, he was a huge disappointment, as he only seemed to have eyes for his wife and children. Monique wasn't sure how much more of this she could stand. It didn't look like she could ever win him over. Now his selfish wife wanted her to babysit whilst they went out.

But Zoe had said Alan wanted her to babysit, so how could she refuse him? He might even sack her, and she was not ready to go yet, she wanted to do it her way. She scowled. She had no choice really.

"I suppose so," she said, sulkily.

"Many thanks, Monique, you are a star!" said Zoe warmly, but Monique remained cold and distant. Zoe picked up her phone to ring Alan and give him the good news. After she had spoken to him, she came back into the kitchen where Monique was making herself a coffee.

"Oh yes, after you pick up Adam from playschool, I will need the car. I have to go and do some shopping."

"Be my guest," muttered Monique under her breath. That meant she would have to walk to the park this afternoon instead of driving. Ignoring Monique's sullen expression, Zoe went out of the kitchen. She was really looking forward to going out this evening, it had been a while since that had happened.

Chapter Nineteen

Kay had been dubious about how her parents would react to her coming back home after five years. At eighteen she thought she knew everything, and that they were stuffy and old fashioned. All they spoke about was getting a good education, and then being able to find a well paid job. But she had other ideas. She didn't like school, but she did like partying.

By the time she reached eighteen, she had dropped out of sixth form, and had absolutely no idea what she would do in the future. Then one night she came in late, she had been drinking, and her dad was angry because she had borrowed his car, and was clearly over the limit. Luckily for them both, she had not been stopped that night, but Nigel had really read his daughter the riot act, calling her a waste of space, and other uncomplimentary criticisms. Her mother, Penny, had tried to calm the situation down, but the next day, when they were both at work, Kay packed her belongings and left home.

She had started off in London, staying with a friend, until her friend's mother got tired of the situation. She was asked to leave, and that was the end of that friendship. She then had the idea of going to the coast, where it was cheaper to live and, during the summer, she could get work. She didn't really want to work, but she realised she could not survive without money.

So she had spent the past five years working her way around the Kent coast, starting off at Whitstable. She had worked in a cafe near to the beach, and her boss allowed her to occupy the bedsitter above the property. It was damp and had no heating, so when winter arrived she moved on to Margate. She worked in shops and snack bars; washing up, clearing tables, and all the menial tasks. By now she was realising her parents had been right, and she needed a good job.

She had been offered the bedsitter at Ramsgate. It was no worse than anywhere else she had stayed. In fact, in the summer, she could open the window, and it looked out onto a small garden with decking. It was nice to sit out there in the summer, but it was an old building, so it was cold in winter, as it didn't have modern amenities such as central heating.

Monique was also living in a bedsitter in Ramsgate, which was how she met her. She had previously been in an equally dingy bedsitter in Paris, but had trained to be a child carer, and taken her exams to get qualifications.

When the two young women commiserated with each other about their positions, they made a pact to help each other to get a nanny job. Monique had told her she had just lost one, and not only that, she had miscarried, and Kay could not help being sorry for her. At the time those were the only details that she knew.

Then Kay heard that Stephen Ward was living in Broadstairs with his wife, and her first baby was due soon. She had always admired him as an author, and read many of his romantic fiction works, becoming transported into a world where love conquers all. It was such an escape from real life.

Kay had then taken the trouble to get to know Chloe, and had managed to put the idea of having a nanny into her head. Once Monique had written Kay glowing references, Chloe couldn't wait for her to start.

When it was Kay's turn to help Monique with a reference, she was only too glad to oblige. But, soon after that, everything started to go wrong. Chloe's death turned everything upside down, and then she found out that Monique was working for the policeman who was investigating Chloe's murder. Moving into the house had not helped, and lately Monique seemed to be getting more and more erratic and wild in her behaviour, so Kay decided it was time to go home where she hoped she would be safe.

She had kept in touch with her parents with birthday and Christmas cards, but did not visit them, as she had not achieved much. Her idea was to make a lot of money, and then go back one day and show them how well it had turned out for her, but this had not happened. She had come crawling back with her tail between her legs, telling them very little about why she was back. But they had still welcomed her with open arms, and not asked many questions, and it was clear to see how much they had missed her. She did have feelings of guilt, and wished now that she had not run away, but stayed in her home town and got the education she could have had, and maybe even gone to university.

She had forgotten just how big her bedroom had been. It faced south, so after a comfortable sleep on her first night, she woke up to be greeted by the sun streaming in her window. She got up and made herself a cup of tea, then took it back to bed. Both her parents left early to go to work. They both worked at the local hospital. Penny was in the office, but had worked her way up to head of department, and Nigel had started off working in the staff restaurant, but was now head of catering.

At ten o'clock she decided to get up. So she had a shower, and put on a light summer skirt and matching blouse. She opened up her computer, intending to check if there were any jobs. She had to start somewhere, but no doubt it would not be easy. She was interrupted by the doorbell, so she got up and went to answer it, wondering who it could be.

Alan had very much enjoyed his meal out with Zoe. They had opted to go to the Turkish restaurant along Herne Bay seafront, where they could sit and enjoy watching the tide come in. The waves were lapping gently up the beach, and the ancient clock tower glinted in the evening sun.

Zoe had looked great. She was wearing a blue dress, which really accentuated her big baby blue eyes and her blonde bubbly curls. He really was married to a stunner, and going out like this made them both appreciate each other more.

Alan had cream cotton trousers on, and a coffee coloured open necked shirt. Zoe was secretly admiring him, and noticed one or two of the women sitting in the restaurant discreetly eyeing him. She felt a glow of pride inside that he was her husband, her soul mate, and they could tell each other anything.

"Honey, you look gorgeous," he murmured to her, lifting up his glass of wine. "How are you feeling?"

"Do you know, I think I am getting there. We must have the most miserable nanny on the planet, but the more surly she is, the more together I feel I am, and I never thought I would be saying this."

Alan looked at her in amazement. He had not taken much notice of Monique, but whenever he came in she had always greeted him with a smile, and he knew that Adam loved her.

"Oh honey, I had no idea she was putting you through that. We can get another nanny."

Zoe felt her confidence returning. It was like new life surging through her insides. The numb feeling was going, she felt alive again! She leaned over and touched his arm gently.

"Alan, I don't need a new nanny. A couple more weeks, and then I will be ready to take up the reins again. I want to care for my own children. I really won't need her to stay all summer until September."

They were interrupted briefly as the waiter brought out their meal. They had both ordered a chicken dish, which looked succulent, and it was accompanied by a side salad and rice.

"I hope I can eat it all. It looks lush," giggled Zoe.

"Any extras, push in my direction," grinned Alan.

"You are a big boy now, but you still have hollow legs," laughed Zoe. "It's not fair. You can eat what you want, and never put on an inch."

They started to eat their meal, and Alan returned to their previous discussion.

"Monique. Did we promise her a job until September?"

"No, it's what she wanted, and if you remember, I said it would be no longer than September, and maybe even before that."

"Well, that is OK then. We can give her a couple of weeks' notice."

"Of course," said Zoe. "Now let's do this delicious meal justice."

Because it was such a fine evening, they had walked to the

restaurant. It was no more than a mile from their house, and the walk took them along a path which overlooked the beach. They both enjoyed the bottle of wine with their meal, and by the time they left the restaurant to walk home, Zoe was feeling more relaxed than she had for a long time.

When they arrived home, Monique was sitting in the lounge feeding Erica. Her face wreathed into a smile when she saw Alan, but it didn't last long; she glared at Zoe, who did not dare look at Alan in case she giggled.

"Thank you, Monique, I will finish feeding Erica, and you can go to bed."

Monique reluctantly handed Erica over, and Alan felt in his pocket, taking out a fifty pound note that he had recently drawn out.

"It was very kind of you to babysit for us, take this for your trouble," he said, smiling at her. Monique smiled back. This man was just too attractive, and so generous with money. Her morose mood lifted.

"Thank you so much," she said, taking the note and tucking it into her handbag.

Zoe and Alan took Erica into the bedroom with them. She had finished her bottle now, so Zoe winded her, and then lay her down in her cot. "This should keep her happy until about six," she remarked.

"That reminds me, I have an early start," said Alan, climbing into bed. "I am meeting James at seven o'clock in Canterbury."

"You were saying you might have to stay over, so don't forget to put your overnight bag in the car," Zoe reminded him.

It didn't take either of them long to fall asleep, and just as Zoe had predicted, Erica was awake at six o'clock, making it clear how hungry she was. Zoe fed her whilst Alan got himself ready for the journey.

"You should have some breakfast before you leave," she said, anxiously.

Alan grimaced. "It's too early, honey, but I dare say James and I will stop for something on the way there, and it will break up the journey."

"Are you sure you don't want me to do you a packed lunch?"

"I am sure. You have your hands full with Erica."

129

He came over and kissed them both. "I am off now, but if I can get back tonight I will."

"Drive carefully," said Zoe. She would miss him, especially if he stayed overnight, but there was no way she would ever make him feel bad about it. She trusted Alan completely, and knew he would be back as soon as he could.

She watched him go out to the drive and get in the car. She could hear signs of Monique getting up now. The shower was going, and the toilet was flushed, but she didn't expect her to start work until eight o'clock. Alan's car pulled out of the drive and continued down towards the seafront. He would then drive through Herne village and take the main road into Canterbury.

Zoe continued to sit there in her dressing gown winding Erica. She was becoming more awake now, and didn't go back to sleep immediately after feeding. Her head was strong and she held it up whilst nestling against Zoe's shoulder. As Zoe turned her round so she could see her face, Erica's mouth crinkled into a smile. It was the first time Zoe had seen it, and a wave of emotion passed through her. Her baby loved her, she had smiled at her!

After a while, she was satisfied that Erica was comfortable, so she changed her nappy, and then she could hear Adam calling out. Monique appeared from nowhere, dressed and ready to start.

"I will go and get Adam up," she said.

"Thanks," said Zoe. "I am going to lay Erica down now, and then it's time I showered and dressed. But first I need to see Adam."

She walked upstairs and put Erica back into her cot. She was still in her babygrow and would be dressed at her next feeding time. Adam was banging on his baby gate, which was there to keep him safe until he learned to negotiate the stairs safely. She lifted him over, and hugged him tightly.

"So you are awake my big boy. Let's go down the stairs together, and then you can have your breakfast."

She was aware of Monique glowering at her, but she really didn't care. It was only right that Adam saw his mother when he woke up, especially as his dad was at work. She lifted him into his high chair. "There we go, mummy is going to get dressed, and Monique is going to get you some breakfast."

130

She then mounted the stairs, sorting herself a clean towel from the airing cupboard, and turned the shower on.

Alan picked up James outside Canterbury police station. They were both in plain clothes today, as they didn't want to create a stir when they turned up in Yorkshire. The traffic was beginning to get busy with the daily commute, so Alan got onto the A2 and headed towards London.

They kept going for a couple of hours, until the main part of the journey was over, and then stopped at services. The time was now nine-thirty, and Alan estimated that the rest of the journey might take between one or two hours, traffic willing.

"I don't know about you, James. I didn't fancy breakfast earlier, but I could murder a fry-up now."

James brightened visibly. "That sounds good, sir, and a cuppa to go with it."

They sat in the cafe eating their full English, washed down with a couple of mugs of tea.

Alan could feel his energy returning, and after half an hour he was ready to continue the journey.

"Do you think we will find her there, sir? It's a long way to come," said James, cautiously.

"Absolutely, and if she is not, we will find out where she is. I have not come all this way for nothing!" said Alan, firmly.

"We can't rule her out of the murder enquiry unless she has a good reason for doing a runner," remarked James, thoughtfully."

"Exactly, James, this is why we are here," agreed Alan.

They eventually found the road. It had rows of terraced houses, all looking exactly the same. The house was an end of terrace with a tiny front garden and a path leading to the gate, which was shut. Alan opened it carefully, it was a bit rickety, and James followed him through. Alan rang the doorbell, and they both stood looking at the door, and hoping it would be answered.

There was a sound of footsteps inside, and when the door was opened, Kay stood there. But, judging by the look of horror on her face, she was not pleased to see them.

Chapter Twenty

"Good morning, Miss Wilson. Do you remember me, DCI Alan Clarke?" Alan hurried on before she could reply. "This is Detective Constable James Martin with me today. We have come to ask you a few questions."

Kay knew exactly who he was, but had believed that nobody knew her address in Yorkshire. Horror and fear dominated her senses at that moment. Did he know she was friendly with Monique? Had Monique done something dangerous? Was he aware they had both forged each other's references? And what about Stephen and the family she had deserted? She had no idea what to say to them, but she realised, more than ever, she would have to keep herself together, and sound plausible. Whatever would her parents say if she was arrested?

Janet Cross was taking her time in coming out of the house next door. She had always been a nosey neighbour, and the houses were close to each other. Kay made a supreme effort to act normally.

"Good morning, Janet. Do come in gentlemen."

"Oh, so you are back then?" Janet stared at them all.

Alan and James went into the hall, and Kay shut the door firmly.

"Sorry about her, she has always been very nosey," she explained.

They stood waiting to be invited further, but the invite was not forthcoming. Clearly Kay Wilson did not want them to stay for long. But Alan had not driven for over four hours just to spend a few minutes here; he wanted to take his time. He smiled kindly at her.

"May I call you Kay?"

She nodded.

"We have driven here from Canterbury. The family you left so suddenly are concerned about you, and hope you are not in any sort of trouble. So James and I would like to sit down with you and discuss exactly what has been going on."

Kay looked at him. He had a pleasant manner, and did not look angry. Maybe he had literally just come to check that she was OK, and genuinely didn't know about her connection with Monique or that they had forged each other's references.

"If you go and sit in the front room, I can make you some tea or coffee. I know it's a long drive here."

"Thank you, milk and two sugars in the tea please, for both of us," said Alan. He winked at James, who was a little bemused. "Got to get her on side," he whispered, confidentially, whilst she was in the kitchen.

Kay returned to the front room a few minutes later with the tea and a packet of chocolate digestives. "Oh, my favourites," beamed Alan, and Kay started to relax, it seemed like she was safe.

James set up his phone to record the interview, and Alan explained what would happen. Kay nodded, and then watched them whilst they drank their tea and ate some biscuits.

Kay was feeling much more relaxed now, which is what Alan had intended. He wiped biscuit crumbs from his mouth, and nodded at James to start recording the interview.

"Where are your parents, Kay?"

"At work. They both work at our local hospital."

"They obviously know that you worked for Stephen Ward, and that his wife was murdered, I take it?"

"I did explain when I came home. They are glad that I am home now."

"Of course they are. Now, tell me exactly why you left?"

Kay noticed that Alan's manner had become very serious now. He was watching her very carefully, and, as she met his eyes, she knew he would be very hard to tell lies to.

"When I first went there, it was a great job. Stephen is such a nice man, and Chloe was very welcoming. Then, after she died, Stephen shut himself away, and I started to wonder who had murdered her and why. The house became creepy to me, so I decided I wanted to come home where I felt safe."

Alan studied her carefully. She didn't fully meet his gaze. She looked uncomfortable, and he was sure she was hiding something.

"I can understand you wanting to come home to your parents, but why did you move in there out of your flat as soon as Chloe died?"

"Because Stephen was devastated, and he had no idea how to care for Luke. Until he met Chloe he was a confirmed bachelor, with no experience of young children."

"Do you not think he is devastated that you have left?"

"He probably is, and yes, I do feel guilty, and I miss Luke, but I hope he will quickly find another nanny."

Remembering what James had discovered about the nanny agency, Alan phrased his next question carefully, and keenly watched her reaction.

"Did you come from the nanny agency with good references, as I would imagine nobody would employ a nanny without them?"

Kay felt like his eyes could see right inside her, and would know if she was lying, so she dodged the question as best she could.

"Yes, Chloe was very impressed with my references."

Alan's demeanour changed instantly. He was not a man to be messed with!

"But you didn't come from an agency, did you, Kay? The agency confirmed that you didn't have the necessary qualifications, and they told you they could not have you on their books until you did the course and earned them," he barked at her.

Panic rushed through Kay. She felt sick inside, and had no idea how she would get out of this. If he found out about Monique, and realised he also had a nanny working for him with a false reference, it just didn't bear thinking about. She had to give the performance of her life to make him believe her, otherwise she could see herself being taken back to Canterbury police station.

She gave a loud sob, and reached for the box of tissues, wailing. "OK, I admit it. I forged my own references, and made up a family names and addresses. I got to know Chloe, and then I showed her the references." She then let out more sobbing noises, with tears running down her cheeks.

Alan was about to remind her it was a criminal offence, but women's tears had always made him feel uncomfortable. Kay could see he was a little uncertain.

"I would have told you anyway. There was no need to bully me," she said, wiping her eyes.

"Excuse me, I don't bully anyone," said Alan. "Maybe you don't realise how much time and money it's costing to come here and find out why you ran away. You should have done it the proper way, and given notice."

Kay knew he was right. There was no excuse for the way she had run out in his eyes, but sheer panic over the loose cannon that was Monique had been the reason, and she could never tell him that.

"I am sorry I didn't give notice. I was worried that Stephen might try and talk me out of it."

Alan had not finished with her yet. There were still more questions, and she seemed calmer now.

"How did you get on with Anna?"

"OK. As you know, she was Chloe's close friend. She didn't like Stephen at first, but when she got to know him she realised he is a decent man."

"So you think that about him, too?"

"Oh yes, he lives in his own world a bit. He likes nothing better than being in his study writing. He told me once that writing love stories with a happy ending gives him an inner peace."

"I think you were attracted to Stephen. You took the job so you could be near to him, am I right?"

Kay could feel herself blushing because she knew it was true, but the conversation was not heading the right way, and she knew it.

"I am attracted to the lovely stories he writes, show me a woman who isn't. But Chloe was his wife, and they made a very attractive couple," she said indignantly.

"Then along comes Anna, and you feel usurped," said Alan, pointedly.

His words annoyed Kay a lot. His attitude was really getting to her. All this probing into her innermost thoughts and her private life.

"After Chloe died, it got me thinking, who had killed her and why? She was a very sweet person, but somehow vulnerable because she worried about a birthmark, and yet if she looked in the mirror, she was so beautiful. "

"So did you leave because you thought Stephen had killed her?" persisted Alan.

"No, absolutely not. He is kind and sensitive. I saw how patient he was with her mood swings. I never thought it was Stephen."

"Well who did you think it was then?"

"I have lain awake at night trying to puzzle it out, but it casts doubts on everyone connected with her. Anna and Richard Lyon for example."

"What do you know about Richard?" asked Alan, curiously.

"Very little. He keeps himself to himself, but Anna told me he has been friends with Stephen since university days. He is a gay man, and until a couple of years ago, his partner had lived with him for ten years. His name was Ed, he was only thirty, and he committed suicide.

This information made Alan's ears prick up. He would have to find out more about this.

"Do you know what caused him to do this?"

"No, it's been hushed up. Richard doesn't want people to know, but Stephen told Anna in confidence."

"I see." Alan made a mental note to interview Anna again, she obviously couldn't be trusted if she had betrayed a confidence.

"Well Kay, we are going back to Canterbury to inform everyone concerned that you are safe and well with your parents. I must impress on you that we may still need you to help with our enquiries, so do not go abroad, or anywhere else without informing me at Canterbury Police. And don't try forging any references again. It is a criminal offence, and make no mistake about it, you will face charges."

Kay held her breath. They really were going now, but she had to warn Monique to keep her mouth shut, and not to do anything to attract attention. Would she ever be able to breathe easy again, or would this all still be hanging over her? She could tell that Alan Clarke suspected she had killed Chloe. He had even tried to accuse her, but hopefully he would now go and investigate Richard and Anna.

136

"Yes, I understand. I will be here with my parents for the foreseeable future."

James ended the recording, and she saw them both out of the house. Thank goodness her parents were not there to hear all that. She watched at the window until she saw the car drive down the road. Then she picked up her phone and texted Monique, she had to warn her.

'MONIQUE IT'S KAY, DONT TELL ANYONE YOU KNOW ME. POLICE HAVE BEEN HERE TODAY.'

"Well James, what do you make of her?" asked Alan, as they were driving towards home.

"I think she had designs on Stephen after Chloe died, and that is why she moved in, and then Anna came along and messed up all her plans, so she came home in a huff."

"She might have killed Chloe so she could have Stephen. We can't rule her out and, like the others, she has no alibi for that night, she reckons she was at her flat alone."

James laughed. "Let's face it, sir, all these women seemed to want Stephen Ward. Anna has also taken a shine to him, and she could have murdered Chloe, too."

"Hell hath no fury," muttered Alan. "It looks like we can make it back tonight James, if I step on it."

"Sounds good to me, sir," said James, settling back in his seat.

Chapter Twenty-one

Zoe felt as if her night out with Alan had done her good. It had been a while since they had gone out. When she was pregnant she had been happy to stay at home, and after a day of looking after Adam, she usually found herself dozing off on the sofa. But it was amazing how a meal at a local restaurant had really lifted her spirits.

She busied herself after Alan had gone by putting the washing on. Adam was at playschool, and Monique would go and pick him up about twelve. There was an awkward silence between them. She had tried asking Monique about her life before she came to England, but she said very little, only that she had a bedsitter in Paris, and had no family living. Zoe felt sorry for her with no family, maybe that was why she was so morose. She decided to try harder with her. Monique had been a good nanny with the children, no complaints there, and she didn't want to part with bad feelings.

During the morning her mother rang her, and she told Ruth that Alan had gone up to Yorkshire for the day. "So you are on your own?" enquired Ruth.

"Well, Monique is here with me, of course," said Zoe, smiling in her direction. She had her phone on loudspeaker, so Monique could hear the conversation.

"Come and meet me at Whitstable Castle. We can have afternoon tea, and bring the babies, of course," said Ruth.

"Oh, that does sound nice. Does three o'clock sound about right?" asked Zoe.

"Perfect," said Ruth, and then her phone clicked off.

Zoe turned round and smiled at Monique.

"You can have a couple of hours off, if you like, this afternoon Monique. I am meeting my mother for afternoon tea."

Just at that moment Monique's phone buzzed, and when she picked it up, the blood drained from her face as she read Kay's urgent message in capital letters.

"Are you OK?" asked Zoe, with genuine concern.

Monique had to think quickly before this all blew up in her face. She had taken this job because she wanted Alan. She also wanted his children, especially Erica, because holding her in her arms made up slightly for her own loss; the baby that she had miscarried had been a girl. But she could never forget the experience of having to deliver a baby that she knew had already died. She had no one to turn to help her with her grief. The father was a married policeman. He would not leave his wife, and he had treated her just like a plaything, to be picked up and dropped whenever he fancied.

Monique knew that Alan would never treat her like that. He treated Zoe like a queen. She had come to realise that their marriage was solid and she could never break them up, so there was only one thing left for her now. She knew Zoe was getting better, and would not need her soon; but Erica needed her, she had to take this baby and run. In her mind, Erica was her baby, she belonged to Monique.

"It's a message from Paris saying my uncle has died suddenly. I will have to go back tomorrow. I am so sorry."

Zoe felt relief sweep through her. That meant she would not have to give Monique notice. It was all going to turn out for the best. Monique had said she had no relatives, but maybe she didn't count her uncle.

"Oh Monique, I am so sorry to hear that. I fully understand. We will pay for you to fly back if that helps."

"You are very kind," said Monique, with a ghost of a smile. "I will pack this afternoon."

"Yes, you can do it whilst we are out," said Zoe, happily.

"Can I ask just one more thing?" said Monique.

"Of course, anything."

"Can you leave Erica with me this afternoon. I would like to feed her once more, and it will be easier for you and your mother in the teashop."

Zoe smiled, and her heart warmed towards Monique. She really did love the children, especially baby Erica.

"Of course, Monique, and don't worry, we will give you a great reference for your next family. You have been an excellent nanny."

"Thank you. I think it's time for me to go and get Adam now," said Monique.

Zoe went to hang the washing on the line. Whilst she was out in the garden her thoughts turned to Monique, and she wished she had been more patient with her. The girl had proved her worth as a nanny, the very least she could do was to let her look after Erica for one last time.

Alan left most of the bill paying to Zoe. He always joked about it, and called her his secretary. They had always paid Monique in cash. She had said she preferred her money that way, and although she had only worked a week of her current month, Zoe wanted her to have a month's money, and maybe even a bonus because she wanted to show her how grateful she was for the help that Monique had given her at such a difficult time.

So she left earlier in the afternoon, knowing that the bank closed at three o'clock. Adam held her hand and trotted into the bank whilst she drew out a thousand pounds. She reckoned that would tide Monique over until she managed to get another job. Then she drove on to Whitstable Castle to meet her mother.

Ruth was sitting in the cafe, which overlooked the beautiful castle grounds, sipping a cup of tea. Zoe put her arms around her and hugged her. "Hi Mum. Great to see you."

Ruth gave her a worried look. "Where is Erica?"

"It's OK, Mum, I left her with Monique. It's her last day. She is going back to Paris tomorrow."

Ruth pushed her cup away and jumped up. "I couldn't tell you on the phone this morning, as I knew Monique would hear me. I have disturbing news about your nanny, and we must go back to your house now. Erica might be in grave danger!"

Zoe's face went white; it couldn't be true. Ruth took charge of the situation.

"Get into my car, we can come back for yours later. I have Adam's seat in the back of mine."

Zoe didn't argue. She quickly lifted Adam and strapped him into his baby seat in the back of the car. Her mother had already started the engine, so Zoe jumped in beside her and buckled up her seat belt.

Ruth was trying to keep calm as she was driving. It would not do to have an accident, but she owed Zoe an explanation. She drew a deep breath.

"I haven't been much use to you since Erica was born, I know, it's been so busy at the b and b."

"Mother, you have your own life too. Now just tell me what is wrong!"

"I was at my keep fit class, and the girls were talking. Evidently a policeman who lives in Whitstable had a nanny named Monique, it was rumoured he had an affair with her, although not proved. She was fired, and she was pregnant, then she lost the baby. Apparently the police spoke to her because the wife had an accident, she fell down the stairs, but no charges were actually made, although the girl is understood to be suffering from mental problems."

"But Mum, how do you know it's my Monique?" asked Zoe, but she could feel fear spreading through her insides, even as she said it. Monique was definitely very attached to Erica, and she had almost felt at times that Monique wanted to take the children over, and that would be the action of a bereaved mother.

"Not for sure," agreed Ruth, but let's get home and make sure our little girl is safe."

They had reached Herne Bay now, and only needed to drive up the hill, so Ruth avoided the High Street and drove the car up Beacon Road which ran along the downs.

"Did an agency supply her?" asked Ruth, as she negotiated the hill. There were cars parked over one side, and she had to slow up to let a couple of cars past that were coming down the hill.

"No, they didn't have anyone at the time. We advertised online, and when she came round she had the most wonderful reference."

Ruth was silent, she knew at the time Zoe had been very unwell and depressed, so it was understandable that Alan had wanted to get someone quickly. But Zoe felt guilty.

"Oh Mum, what have I done? It's all my fault!"

Ruth pulled into the drive. Zoe's heart was beating so fast, she felt it would burst through her chest. But she had not forgotten that Adam was in the car, and was already calling out. "Why we come home?" he had been expecting afternoon tea.

"Mum, you are going to stay out here with Adam, and I will go in and see what is happening."

"I am going to call the police!" said Ruth grimly.

Zoe pulled at her arm. "No Mum, promise me you won't. Monique is not very well. Let me handle the situation, that is if she is still there."

"I will only give you five minutes!" said Ruth firmly. Now was not the time for Zoe to play the good Samaritan, her baby might be in danger.

Zoe jumped from the car, and slowly approached the front door. She could feel her heart beating so fast; it was a fear of the unknown. She had no idea what to expect. She found her front door key, and opened door. The hall was empty, but she thought she could hear a sound from the kitchen. The kitchen door was open, and when she got near to it, she noticed it was ajar. She heard the faint cry of a baby, and as she looked, she saw Monique holding Erica very close to her, and next to her was a suitcase on wheels.

Monique reacted very quickly, turning towards Zoe with a bread knife in her hand, and a very strange look in her eyes. "Keep away, or I will use this," she said, brandishing it in front of her.

Zoe's reaction even took herself by surprise. Suddenly, without warning, that feeling of emotion that binds mother and baby hit her like a bolt from the blue. The numbness had gone, replaced by fear at what might happen to her baby girl. She was a tigress protecting her cub, and she knew in that moment she would die herself rather than let anyone harm a hair of her baby's head.

Chapter Twenty-two

Monique had spent the rest of the morning planning her escape. She guessed that Zoe would be out no longer than a couple of hours with her mother. Adam usually had his tea about five. In fact, she might even be back before then. Tea time and bath time were always quite hectic, and sometimes Alan was back to be involved in it. But Zoe had said he was travelling up north today, and might not even be back until tomorrow, so this seemed the best time to go.

One thing was for sure, she was not going back to Paris. She never wanted to set foot in that bedsitter again, she was going to start a new life with Erica somewhere safe, where nobody would ever find her. She was not even going abroad. There was a little village in the Scottish Highlands, it was so far behind the times, the people there didn't even have TV sets. They also minded their own business. She had spent a holiday there last year, so she knew she could rent a tiny cottage for a very low rent. She planned to change her name, and maybe her hairstyle and colour too. She was so determined to create a new life for herself and Erica, that nothing was going to stop her.

That bedsitter in Paris held so many bad memories for her. She had never known her father. It had been just Monique and her mother. Right from a young child, she had seen her mother drinking until she couldn't stand up, and when she was short of money, there was an endless procession of men visiting the bedsitter. She had tried not to watch her mother degrading herself, but there was not another room to escape to.

Then, at the age of eight, her mother had the idea of using Monique in her sex games. But even at that young age, Monique refused, she knew it was wrong. When she was at school, she mixed with girls from normal, loving families, then visited them as often as she was invited. Her shame about her mother, and the life she led, kept her from confiding to anyone, it was her shameful secret, and it was locked away inside her.

Monique liked going to school, and she worked hard because she wanted a better life. She knew at the age of eleven that she wanted to work with children. She had the initiative to start doing babysitting for the parents of her friends from the age of fourteen. This gave her a little bit of money, which helped her to survive, as her mother rarely bought any food.

She had left school at sixteen and come to England. She would have liked to continue her education and get qualifications, but life with her drunken mother was unbearable. All this had affected her mental state. All Monique wanted was to be loved, but she had never received any from her mother.

Monique managed to get into college in London, and was able to board there, and that is when she got her childcare qualifications. The nanny agency covered the whole of the UK, and were happy to have her on their books. When they had found her the job with the policeman and his family, she was so happy. He had five year old twin boys, and Monique bonded with them immediately.

The man was a very high profile figure in the police force. His status gave him a sense of power, and it was not long before he started an affair with Monique. She could not have resisted him if she wanted to, he was a man that never took no for an answer. It wasn't long before she realised she was not getting the love she craved so much. Her emotions were all over the place, and one day, whilst his wife was talking down to her as if she was a menial rather than the nanny they had entrusted their children to, Monique put her foot out as she was going down the stairs.

The fall was serious enough for her to break her leg, so she had to rely heavily on Monique to help with the children. Her last memory of the policeman was the day he told her she was just a bit on the side and meant nothing to him, and as if to prove this fact, he raped her.

Monique realised this life was turning her into a very unstable person, and then she found out she was pregnant. She finally had someone to love, but her boss then sacked her and, at five months, she was given the devastating news that her baby was dead; there was no heartbeat. So she had to go into hospital and be induced so she could give birth to it.

She could still remember the pain when she held her tiny little girl in a special casket that had been made for babies who had been miscarried. She was so tiny, yet she looked perfect, and Monique was so full of grief, but had no one to share it with.

After that she had come to Ramsgate, and this was where she had met Kay, and they had done their best to help each other. But, upon reflection, it had not helped either of them as they had both been forced into a position where they had had to change their lives.

Monique had enjoyed her short time at this house. She loved the children, and was incredibly jealous of Zoe. This is why it felt right to her to take Erica. Zoe didn't love Erica, but she did, and they would start a new life together.

Within fifteen minutes of Zoe leaving the house, Monique had packed her few meagre belongings, and then she prepared a bag of things that Erica would need. She had booked a train ticket to Scotland online, and luckily there was a train up to London just after three-thirty that would take her to Victoria Station, and she could then get a tube. After travelling overnight, and some changes, she would arrive at the village in the morning, so would have all that day to find somewhere to stay.

She picked up Erica to give her a bottle before they left. She was such a good baby, she fed and then went back to sleep. Monique looked down at her, and she could feel her heart glow with love for this tiny being. She knew she would always take great care of her.

It was just after three, so she collected her suitcase from the kitchen, and put Erica into her papoose, strapping it safely to her body. But the unmistakable odour of her nappy assaulted Monique's senses, so she unstrapped the papoose, and laid Erica on a kitchen towel, intending to change her nappy.

g

It was then she heard the front door open. Suddenly all her hopes were going to be dashed, there was someone there to stop her. Without even thinking about it rationally, she clasped Erica to her, and with her other hand she picked up the bread knife, and held it out as Zoe entered the kitchen. She had learned the hard way, over the years, that the best means of defence was attack. As soon as she saw the horror on Zoe's face, she realised that Zoe would think she was going to harm Erica; but she would never hurt her, the knife was to stop Zoe from coming near, and to dissuade her from making an attempt to grab Erica.

Zoe felt sick inside when she saw the knife. It was inches away from her precious sleeping baby. But during her years as a nurse, she had been in this position before. She had learned to deal with people who had mental health issues. She had once talked a man down from the hospital roof where he had been intent on taking his own life.

However this was personal, this was her beautiful daughter. She was emotionally involved in every way, so to keep Erica safe, she had to control the fear and panic which was running amok inside her.

Keeping her voice low and calm she started to speak to Monique. She kept her tone warm, she knew she must not make her angry, and she tried to ignore the banging of her heart, which seemed to be working overtime.

"Monique, you don't need the knife. Nobody is going to attack you. How about you hand it over to me, and then we can sit down and talk about what is troubling you."

Monique was expecting her to be angry, and shout at her. The kindness in her voice brought tears to her eyes; nobody had ever cared about her before. Why was Zoe being so kind to her, she had her baby, she should be angry?"

"You don't love Erica, you never have. I am taking her to a new life. The knife will keep you away from me whilst I come past."

Zoe realised that, as far as Monique was concerned, it was a very hopeless situation. Firstly it would not be long before her mother came bursting in, and there was no way Monique would be able to escape with Erica, a suitcase and the knife. She just didn't have enough hands.

"Monique, you and I are not too different, you know. I have been suffering from mental problems since Erica was born, but today I found myself recovering, and I know I will cope. I believe you are also suffering for whatever reason. Maybe it's because you are on your own in a strange country, I don't know, but there is definitely something wrong."

The result of her words was to cause Monique to burst into tears. She was not used to anyone being kind to her, all she had ever known was emotional abuse. Zoe walked slowly towards her, knowing this girl was not dangerous, she was ill. She gently took the knife out of Monique's hand, and with a sob, Monique handed Erica to her, then bent her body to the ground and sobbed her heart out.

Zoe was moved by her. This was genuine, and she knew what she needed to do. She took Erica to the front door, and her mother appeared out of the car, with Adam crying and making his voice heard from the back seat.

"Mother, take the children back to yours. I will come and pick them up later," she said.

"What's going on?" asked Ruth, feeling very bewildered.

"I will tell you later," promised Zoe, who then went back into the house where Monique was sitting on the floor still sobbing. She picked her up and held her until the sobbing stopped, and she was still. Her tear-stained face was red and blotchy, and Zoe's heart went out to her.

"Right, I am going to put the kettle on, and then you are going to tell me what this is all about," she said firmly to her. After the kettle had boiled, Zoe made her a cup of coffee, and they sat down together.

Monique poured her heart out to Zoe. She told her about her life in Paris, and why she had left home. She then went on to explain how she had taken the courses needed to be a nanny, and Zoe could see why she loved children so much. Monique needed love, and she could give it to children, and they would love her back. She felt so sad for her, that her life had been so empty.

Then Monique told her about the policeman she had worked for and how he had treated her, which positively sickened Zoe. Nobody should be treated like that.

"I do know about this man, Monique. It is nothing to do with Alan, as he belongs to a different branch, but he has been arrested recently, as several women have come out and said he raped them. What he did to you was coercive control, which does not go down well for him in a court of law."

"I threatened to report him, but he laughed at me, and said no one would believe me if I did," said Monique.

"Well, if you feel up to it, you can add your voice to the others he has abused, and he will get the punishment he deserves!" said Zoe angrily. It sounded like this girl had been used and abused for all of her life.

Monique looked at her gratefully. She knew she had treated Zoe badly, yet she had been so kind. Just thinking about it made her feel emotional.

"What will happen to me now?" she asked, anxiously.

"I work at the QEQM, when I am not having babies, that is," laughed Zoe. "If you let me take you there, I have colleagues who can help you. I believe you are still suffering from the trauma of losing your baby. But I promise you, there are people to give you help and support. Will you come with me?"

Monique had fully expected to be arrested. She was a criminal, she had not expected the kindness that Zoe had shown towards her. But it was like balm to her in her confused mental state. Unbelievably, Zoe seemed to understand her, and wanted to help her. She did want to get well again. She knew she was not well, but this was the first bit of kindness she had ever known. The idea of going to hospital and getting help was a comforting one. She had never known the love of a mother, but Zoe felt like a caring person, and she totally trusted her.

"Why are you being so kind to me?" She said wonderingly. "I have done bad things, and I don't deserve it."

Zoe put her arm gently around her. "Monique, you do deserve it, you deserve respect and understanding. Like you, I have had mental health problems, but I haven't had a life like yours where nobody cared about you or gave you any support. I believe you can get better with the right help. There are good people at the hospital who can help you get your life back on track."

"I trust you, Zoe, and I want to get well. I will come to the hospital with you."

"That is good news," said Zoe, linking her arm through Monique's. Then she remembered her car was not outside. But they had come so far, and she was determined not to be thwarted.

"I am just going to call a taxi to take us there."

Chapter Twenty-three

Alan got caught in traffic on the way back. The schools were coming out and cars seemed to be parked everywhere, so he had to negotiate his way carefully, and, to his disappointment, he did not reach the motorway until four-thirty.

"I don't think we will be back much before eight, regrettably," he said.

"Never mind, sir, we will be glad in the morning that we are home," said James.

The traffic was moving quite well on the motorway now, so Alan was able to drive at a steady pace. He heard the notification that a text had come into his phone, but it wasn't possible to stop at the moment. He guessed it might be from Zoe. She wasn't sure if he would be coming home, so it would be quite nice to surprise her. By the time he got home, Adam would probably be fast asleep, and Zoe would have already eaten, but that didn't matter, he couldn't wait to see her, and snuggle up to her when they went to bed.

James was not married, so there would not be anyone at home waiting for him. He did have a girlfriend, but as yet they didn't live together.

"After you drop me, I am going to pick up some fish and chips," said James. "My stomach feels as though my throat has been cut!"

Alan suddenly realised that it was hours since they had eaten. The cooked breakfast had been early this morning, and then the coffee and biscuits had been about midday. He had been so engrossed in the interview with Kay, and then the realisation that they could make it back tonight, he had not paid attention to his stomach, but since James had mentioned fish and chips, he could now feel it loudly grumbling, and he felt really weary.

"No need for that, James. We can stop at services halfway and get something. Another half an hour later won't make much difference."

James visibly brightened. "What a good idea, sir, we seem to be making quite good time now."

"Well, to be honest, James, after our early start, and all this driving, I feel shattered. Some food and a hot drink will give me the energy to drive home."

"I can imagine, sir. Would you like me to have a turn at the wheel."

"No, it's OK, James. Now my stomach knows it hasn't got to wait all night I can manage, but thanks for offering."

Alan continued along the motorway. Most of the traffic seemed to be going in the opposite direction to them, and he was able to coast along comfortably. They arrived at a services at six o'clock, so he parked the car, and they went inside. It was a relief to stretch their legs, and visit the toilets and wash their hands.

There were various food outlets. McDonald's, Fish and Chips, Thai food, and Indian curries. But since James had mentioned fish and chips, they both decided to have that option. They washed it down with large coffees, and Alan was already feeling much better.

He glanced at his watch, it was now six forty-five. "Shall we get going now, James?"

"Good idea, sir," agreed James, and they went outside and got into the car.

The rest of the journey home passed without incident, and Alan dropped James outside the police station, to collect his car, at eight o'clock.

"Thanks for coming with me, James."

"No worries, sir. Now you have a couple more people to interview, Anna and Richard Lyon. It's getting interesting," said James.

"Well, let's say it's getting more involved," groaned Alan. Right now he wanted to forget about who might have killed Chloe, just until tomorrow. He wanted to get home to his family. He watched James walk over to his car, and then took his phone out of his pocket. Across the screen was a message from Zoe, she had left it whilst they were travelling.

'NOT SURE IF YOU ARE BACK TONIGHT ALAN, BUT BABIES ARE WITH MUM, AND I HAVE TAKEN MONIQUE TO HOSPITAL. WILL EXPLAIN WHEN I SEE YOU. XXX'

Alan was gobsmacked. He had gone away for just one day, and whatever had happened? Monique must have had some sort of accident, surely? She was only young, so it couldn't be a serious illness.

He felt concern for Monique. Maybe she had crashed the car, but it seemed like his precious babies were OK.

It would take him about twenty minutes to get home, but if Zoe wasn't there, maybe he should drive over to Whitstable and pick up the little ones. Ruth and Gerald had a business to run, so it might be awkward for them in the morning having the babies to get up and feed. They had breakfasts to cook for the guests. He sent a text back to Zoe, hoping that although she was at the hospital she would see it.

'JUST GOT YOUR TEXT, SO AM OFF TO WHITSTABLE TO PICK UP OUR BABIES. HOPE YOU ARE HOME SOON AND MONIQUE IS OK. XXX'

He then put the car into gear, and headed towards Whitstable.

Zoe had done as much as she could for Monique. The doctor had suggested that a short stay in hospital would be helpful, and she would be put on a course of medication to help her anxiety and instability. He had told them both that Monique was suffering from a mental breakdown, but there were medicines that could really help her. She would also have the option of seeing a psychiatrist.

Monique had been rather horrified to hear this, but Dr Sheridan had assured her that nobody thought she was going mad, and talking to an expert about her worries and fears could really help her. She had been calmer after hearing this, especially when he had assured her that nobody was going to make her do anything. It was entirely up to her if she wanted to accept the help that had been offered.

After having been emotionally neglected throughout her life, this was all quite a shock to Monique. Firstly, the kindness Zoe had shown towards her, and nothing had been mentioned to the doctor about her picking up the bread knife. She felt ashamed to think she had done that. She was out of her mind at that moment, so yes, she knew she did need help, and she did want to get well again.

"I do want to get well," she said, looking at Zoe.

"Well, if you are happy to stay here for a few days, I can come to the ward you will be in, and tomorrow I can bring the things that you need," suggested Zoe.

"Yes, why don't you take Monique there and help her settle in," said Dr Sheridan. He smiled at Monique. "Zoe knows everyone here. She will see you are OK."

Monique nodded, and Zoe took her arm gently. "Right, my friend Lucy works in that ward, you will like her. Let's go and get you sorted."

Zoe went back to reception to see if she could get herself a taxi home. It was now eight o'clock. She sat down and got her phone out, and then saw Alan's text. He was on his way to Whitstable, but if he came over here and picked her up, they could go there together. She rang him, but realised he would be driving and might not be able to pick up.

When Alan saw her name flash up, he wasted no time in pulling over. He was heading up Sturry Hill on his way to the Thanet Way.

"Alan, can you come to the QEQM and pick me up now? I haven't got the car."

"Why not, honey? What's going on?"

"Tell you when I see you. I will wait in the reception area of casualty."

" OK, I'll be as quick as I can."

Alan went round the roundabout where the new houses had been built at Sturry Hill, and proceeded down towards the level crossing, then turned left, driving towards Thanet. It was gone eight o'clock, and here he was now heading towards the hospital. What a day it had been, and it wasn't over yet. It was going to be closer to nine o'clock before they got to Whitstable. But it sounded like a lot had been going on today and, when Zoe saw him, she would tell him all about it.

Luckily there was not much traffic going towards Thanet, and he managed to get to the hospital by eight-thirty. Zoe had been watching for him to arrive, and she came out of the casualty waiting room when she saw him, so he didn't need to park.

She jumped in the car, and put her arms around him and kissed his cheek. "Oh, Alan, I am so pleased to see you. It's been quite a day."

"It certainly has!" agreed Alan. "Where to now?"

"Whitstable. Mum says both the babies are asleep, but Erica will definitely wake up later for a feed, so she suggests I stay the night."

Alan could think of nothing worse than dropping Zoe off at her mother's and then going home to an empty house. Then tomorrow he would not see any of them until the evening. He was feeling tired and a little bit techy.

"What about me?" he said, wearily.

"Darling, you can stay too, of course, as long as you don't mind being in that small bedroom with not much room."

Alan visibly brightened. "I don't mind anything as long as I am with you."

Zoe touched his shoulder gently. He was just like a little boy at times.

Whilst she was sitting waiting for him, she had been debating how she would be able to explain about Monique without him bringing his policeman side into the conversation. Alan was very protective towards his children, so the thought that Monique was trying to abduct Erica, and holding a carving knife in her hand, would not go down well with him.

Zoe had known instinctively that it had been a cry for help, and that Monique was not dangerous, and had been proved right, but Alan would not see it that way. They never kept secrets from one another, but for Monique's sake, right now, she was going to be economical with the truth.

154

"Well, honey, do fill me in on what has happened," Alan said.

Zoe explained about Monique getting a text which seemed to be urgent about her uncle, and that she was about to leave the next day.

"But then mother rang, and asked me to meet her at Whitstable Castle for tea. Then Monique asked me if she could feed Erica for one last time, and I realised just how much she loves her, so I only took Adam out with me."

"Well that was OK, surely? She was their nanny," interrupted Alan.

"This is what I thought, but when I met mother, she told me that a nanny called Monique had been working for that high up policeman, you know the one who recently got arrested, there had been rumours of an affair, and his wife had fallen down the stairs, so the nanny was sacked. The way Mum said it, she made it sound as if Erica was in danger, so we all got into Mum's car and she drove home."

"Go on," said Alan. His face looked grim, as Zoe had been expecting.

"I made mother stay in the car whilst I went into the house to check on Erica. It didn't take me long to realise that Erica was not in danger, but Monique was having a nervous breakdown, literally. Alan, she has had such an awful life, neglected by her mother, then that awful policeman took control of her, and even raped her."

"Well, in that case, Zoe, we must try and persuade her to join the others and give evidence."

"I know, I have already said this to her. I asked her if she wanted to go to hospital. She was so distressed, and she is adamant that she wants to get better."

Alan pondered her word; so the nanny had mental problems, and she was fired from her last job.

"Did we find her on the internet?" he mused.

"Yes, the agency could not match anyone at that point."

"So that amazing reference she gave us, surely it wasn't from the policeman if he fired her?

"I think she might have faked it herself."

Alan stiffened with surprise. Now that was a coincidence, two nannies in one day, both faking their own references. Maybe they were friends. His mind whirled on. If Monique had mental problems, could she have killed Chloe? It was another twist to this murder case.

"Has she mentioned a friend by any chance?"

"Not at all. She seems very lonely."

But Alan was now silent with his thoughts. Zoe would only be able to see it with her nurse's head, and would obviously have empathy for Monique. But it was certainly suspicious, and he would have to interview her very shortly.

"How long will she be in hospital?" he asked.

"Hopefully only for a few days, but I think she wants to go back to France, something about an uncle not being well."

"She can't go back until the rape case is settled. I think I will have to interview her soon. You do realise she can't come back to us now."

Zoe gave him a puzzled look. "I know she can't come back to us, of course. But she needs support, and I will see she gets it. But why would you interview her about the rape case? It's not your case."

Alan knew she would ask him this, but some things he could not share with her, especially as she had been acting like Florence Nightingale to this girl. He could not admit she was a murder suspect, but if his hunch was right, Monique and Kay would have a connection.

"Maybe not me, but she definitely can't leave the country at the moment."

They had reached Whitstable by now. It was past nine o'clock, and it had been a long day for them both. "Oh no, I have to explain it all to mother now," said Zoe.

"Just tell her Monique is in hospital after a breakdown, that explains enough," said Alan.

Zoe doubted if that would be enough information for her mother, but she agreed with Alan, that was enough information for tonight. They got out of the car, and walked up to the front door.

Chapter Twenty-four

Alan didn't expect to sleep that well in the small bedroom at Whitstable. The bed was smaller than theirs at home, but being close to Zoe was very relaxing after a hectic day, and he drifted off immediately. The room was too small to accommodate a cot for Erica as well, so she was in a small bedroom next door with the door open, so they could hear every move that she made.

Zoe had fed Erica before they went to bed, but as yet she could not go all night. Alan had sleepily said he would feed her when she woke up. He knew the bottles were in the fridge, and he would heat one of them in the microwave.

But when Erica woke up at four o'clock, and commenced airing her lungs, Alan had just turned over with a grunt and carried on sleeping. Zoe didn't mind, because he had helped her so much in the early weeks, when she felt physically and emotionally exhausted, but that was behind her now. She could finally take care of both of her children, and it was such a relief. Alan had looked absolutely worn out last night, and she was happy to let him sleep on.

They were staying in a part of the house which was on the top floor, and they had a small kitchen and bathroom of their own. Zoe knew her parents would be busy cooking breakfasts for their guests down below, so it was nice to have their own space to start the day.

Alan was running a bit late this morning, but he rang to say he was coming in. Martha would be back and wondering where he was.

James would probably explain it had been a long day. When he arrived, Martha greeted him cheerily.

"Good morning, sir. How did it go yesterday?"

"I will get James in then tell you both," said Alan. He was beginning to realise this was all too close to home if his nanny was involved. But he was not prepared to hand the case over to anyone else.

Martha went off to get some coffee, and Alan buzzed through to James, who picked up his call immediately. "How are you today, James?"

"Pretty shattered, sir. Can't imagine how you must feel."

"Oh, I am OK, nothing a good injection of coffee won't sort," he said, refusing to let his weariness hold him back. Can you pop along to my office? I have something to share with you."

James was intrigued by this, as he thought they had covered everything yesterday, so he wasted no time in getting to Alan's office. Martha arrived with coffees for them all.

"Did you have a nice birthday?" James asked, smiling.

"I did, we went out for a nice meal," said Martha. She could see Alan was deep in thought. He had not even asked her about yesterday, so it must be something important.

They sat on either side of Alan's desk sipping their coffee.

"This case is becoming a nightmare to me. It's just too close to home!" declared Alan.

"How come?" asked James.

"If you remember, yesterday Kay admitted she had faked her own references, and then, on the same day, I come home to find out my nanny has had a mental breakdown, and is in hospital. My wife then told me our nanny had been a victim of the superintendent who was recently arrested because of claims of rape. He fired her, and she said that was why she had to fake her own reference. Now, to have two women both doing this, makes me think they know each other, and helped each other."

"Wow, that is a coincidence!" said James.

"I never remember dates, this is why I carry a diary, and when I checked, Monique didn't start working for us until the 28th of May, and Chloe was murdered on the 24th."

"But why would she kill Chloe. Did she even know her?" asked Martha, mystified.

"This is where you and James come in. I can't interview someone who worked for me, it's a conflict of interest, but you two can. I want to know if she does know Kay, and also if she has an alibi for the 24th May. You will have to go to the QEQM and interview her today. But rest assured, I am not convinced that Kay Wilson is innocent, she took off very quickly without giving any notice."

James and Martha exchanged glances. This was unusual, but necessary.

"In the meantime, if I can borrow Natalie to record the conversation so we have something to work with, today I want to interview Anna, and Richard Lyon, again."

James smiled, knowing that Natalie was in awe of the boss. She would be both excited and nervous to work with him for a day. "Shall I get her over here, sir?"

"Yes please, and then tomorrow we will have a team briefing again, and run through all the suspects. It's been over a month now, and we are no further forward."

"I will arrange that, sir," said Martha. "In the meantime I will contact the QEQM to make sure we can speak to Monique today."

"Thank you," said Alan. "Now I need to contact Richard Lyon and Anna. "We don't want to waste time calling in if they are not at home."

Two phone calls later, he had appointments set up. His tiredness now forgotten, Alan briefed Natalie on what he expected from her during the interviews. She was elated at being asked to work with him, but also very nervous because she wanted to do everything right. Basically all she was doing was sitting in on the interview and recording it. She knew only a little about the case, so Alan would be doing the interviewing, and she would be supporting him.

The doctor who was caring for Monique had not been keen about her being interviewed so soon after being admitted to hospital. So Martha had to explain that it was an urgent murder case, and by interviewing Monique, she could then be eliminated from their enquiries. He reluctantly agreed after that, and an appointment was fixed for midday that same day.

Martha was happy to accompany James, who was a man who got on with his job quietly, and usually got positive results. Some of the younger officers tended to think they knew everything, and could be quite arrogant, but in time that usually wore off when they found out the job was harder than they expected. Having a rapport with the public was a very important part of the job, as it made it much easier when interviewing people, and if they trusted you, they told you more. This was where Alan had always done so well. He knew how to be charming and polite, but he also knew when to become firm and determined to get at the truth. People had respect for him, and they were more likely to confide in him. James tried to emulate this type of approach himself, because he had seen how it worked for Alan. Knowing that they were rather unwelcome visitors, he was determined to get the interview with Monique done as quickly as possible, and to try and keep her as calm as they could.

When they arrived at the hospital they were directed to the part where Monique was being treated. They had to walk down quite a lot of corridors, but eventually they found the ward. Monique was standing out by reception, and immediately James could see that she was very nervous. A staff nurse was standing with her.

"Good morning, we are here to interview Monique," said James, giving them both a pleasant smile.

"Good morning, I am Staff Nurse Amy Collins, and this is Monique."

"Just call us James and Martha," said James, shaking hands.

Amy, who was short and stocky with brown hair tied back from her face, opened a door leading to a small side room.

"Here you are. You can speak to Monique in here, but not for too long."

"Many thanks," said James, politely holding the door open so Martha and Monique could both enter and sit down. It had sofas facing one another, so Monique sat one side, and then he sat on the other with Martha.

"Monique, I am so sorry you are not well. I just want to ask you

160

a few questions, and then we can leave you in peace," he said, smiling gently.

Monique swallowed quickly, she had a feeling she knew what this was about. Something she had said had made them link her with Kay. It was bound to happen, and she had already decided she was not going to lie to the police. No matter what, she needed to tell the truth. She was not going to deny that she knew Kay.

"I will try and help you," she said, falteringly.

"We are trying to find out who killed Chloe Ward. Did you know her?"

Monique shook her head. "No, I never met her."

"How about Kay Wilson, do you know her?"

"Yes, I know Kay."

"Did she tell you that she was running away. She left the family she was working for two days ago without letting anyone know, and is now in Yorkshire with her parents."

"I see, so that is why I could not get hold of her. It just went to answerphone."

James stared fixedly at her. "So, if you didn't know, it sounds like she made a panic decision to leave. Any idea why?"

Monique had guessed exactly why it was. Kay was desperately trying to hide their connection, but she had just admitted that she knew her. "Well, I think somebody went to interview her yesterday, because she sent me a text saying the police were there, and not to tell anyone that I knew her."

"Why do you think she wanted to hide your connection?"

"I think that was my fault. I said some things I did not mean recently, and I had a breakdown, but I do intend to get well. Maybe she just thought knowing me was a liability."

"Thank you, Monique. Now I need to take you back to the evening of Friday 24th May. Can you remember what you were doing?"

Monique looked blank. "I am not sure. That was a few weeks ago."

"If this helps, it was the Friday of the bank holiday weekend."

"Let me think," she puckered up her face and closed her eyes. "Yes, of course. On Thursday 23rd Mr and Mrs Clarke interviewed me, and on Friday Mrs Clarke rang me to say they would like me to start on Tuesday twenty-eighth, after the bank holiday weekend. I met Kay on Friday evening, and I told her I had got the job. "

"Did Kay write your reference?"

Monique couldn't stop her cheeks from reddening. They had been found out, but it was useless denying it. "She did, because my last employer had sacked me."

James could see this had distressed her, so he tried to sound kind. "Thank you for your honesty. I don't need to tell you that is a criminal offence, but I understand you must have been desperate."

"I was."

"Did you do the same for Kay, and write her a references when she went after the job with Stephen Ward?"

"Yes, we both needed a job, so we helped each other."

James nodded, that now explained the connection. "When you met Kay on the evening of the 24th May, where did you go?"

"Just for a walk to Ramsgate Harbour, then we stopped off at a bistro along the top and had a bite to eat."

"Can you remember what time you got back to your flat in Ramsgate?"

"Not that late. About ten, I think, it was just getting dark."

Just at that moment the door opened, and Staff Nurse Amy Colllins popped her head round. "That's enough now, Monique needs to eat some lunch."

James had got enough information for now. Monique had been honest with him, so he nodded at Martha to stop recording. He turned towards Amy. "Many thanks for letting us interview Monique. I hope you soon feel better, Monique. Go and enjoy your lunch."

"Thank you. Goodbye," said Monique, following after the nurse, who smiled back at James and led her away.

When they got outside, James thanked Martha for accompanying him.

"You are welcome. She did not seem traumatised, so you did well," remarked Martha.

"Yes, I did try hard. But two interesting points came up. Monique reckons she has never met Chloe Ward, which we can try checking with Stephen if it's true. The other point is Kay's alibi was she stayed in on the night of the 24th May, whereas Monique has just told us they went to Ramsgate Harbour. I know this because, as I was coming with you today to do the interview, I quickly familiarised myself with all the notes about the case. Kay was interviewed at the same time as Stephen."

"Yes, I do remember," mused Martha. "Alan will be interested to hear that."

They both got into the car and James drove back to the police station. He was finding this case very interesting, and couldn't wait to hear what information Alan and Natalie would have collected during their interviews. But when they arrived back, Alan was still out, so it would have to wait. Now it was time to eat lunch.

Chapter Twenty-five

Richard Lyon had a free morning, so was happy to get the interview done before lunch, and then this afternoon he could concentrate on his patients. He had already instructed his receptionist to buzz him as soon as DCI Clarke arrived, and then to be ready to make some coffee. He had wondered why they were interviewing him again, as he didn't really have anything to add to his previous statement.

The newspapers had been full of the fact that a worker from the Broadstairs' Funfair was helping the police with their enquiries, but after that it had gone quiet. It seemed he had absconded, which definitely sounded as though he had something to hide.

Then a newspaper had got hold of more information. Apparently the man had been in a car accident, and suffered serious injuries, and might not survive. Well apparently he had survived, and was back with the travellers that he lived with, but had not been arrested, so obviously they had not found enough evidence to arrest him.

Richard had been very concerned when he found out that Kay had vanished without a word. Thank goodness Anna had stepped in. Stephen knew nothing about babies, and seemed all over the place. Richard had always been confident in handling babies, having had practice with Margaret's little ones. In fact, during their ten years together, Stephen and Ed had talked about making their relationship permanent, and maybe, with some help from modern medicine, creating their own family.

He tried to shake away thoughts of Ed. It still hurt him deeply, even after two years. Since Ed had passed he had become much closer to Stephen again. If only Stephen could learn how to manage his money. That was the one thing he did not understand about Stephen, he was a wealthy man, so where did it all go?

Amanda, his secretary, was buzzing. He glanced at his watch. Yes, right on the dot, Clarke was here. He buzzed back at her. "Yes, Amanda?"

"DCI Clarke is here."

"Thank you, Amanda, show him in."

He stood up politely as Alan came in, and noticed it was a different policewoman with him.

They shook hands and Alan introduced her as Natalie. Richard invited them both to sit down.

"Would you like tea or coffee?" he enquired, hospitably.

"Coffee please, two sugars," said Alan, and Natalie shook her head, saying she was fine.

Alan waited until Richard's secretary had brought the coffee in, and then explained that Natalie would be recording their conversation. Taking her cue from that, Natalie set her phone. Alan cleared his throat. "I understand that, until two years ago, you had a long term partner of ten years?"

Richard felt annoyed. Why did the police have to dig around in the past? Why couldn't his private life remain just that; it was nobody else's business.

"Ed was my partner for ten years, but I fail to see what it has to do with the murder investigation."

Alan had been expecting him to react this way, but please or offend, he had to understand what sort of character Richard was, and whether there was any chance that he could have killed Chloe. So he ignored the annoyance in Richard's tone of voice.

"How did Ed die? Presumably he was not old."

Richard had hoped this would not come up. Of course, it did sound bad for him, and the police were always looking to swoop down and find someone responsible for a crime. But he was going to make damn sure they didn't pin it on him!

"If you must know, he died from an accidental drugs overdose."

"Drugs?"

165

"Prescription drugs, and before you ask me, no, Ed was not my patient. He did not lead a very happy life before he knew me. When he was a teenager, he realised that he was gay, but he came from a very religious family that did not embrace the fact that he wanted to come out. His parents forbade him to tell anyone because of the shame it would bring to them. So that was when his mental health problems started. When I met him he was an emotional mess, but over the years I was able to give him stability, and he did come out. Unfortunately he came to rely on the medication that was prescribed for him, and he didn't have a great memory. The night he overdosed he had been drinking a bit as well."

"Are you sure he didn't commit suicide?" asked Alan, remembering that this is what Anna had told Kay, although he could not be sure that Anna spoke the truth.

Richard was usually a very quiet but deep man. He didn't share much about his life, but this policeman was not afraid to pull punches, and very hard to deceive; his gaze seemed to bore right into Richard. He knew that all Alan had to do was check the death certificate, and then he would be accused of lying. Inside he was feeling devastated. The only way he had been able to reconcile Ed's death was to believe that it was an accidental drug overdose. Now this policeman, turning up and questioning him so closely, was bringing up all the heartbreak he had tried so hard to put behind him during the last two years.

"The coroner recorded it as suicide because of the amount of medication inside him, but I never believed Ed would do that. He did not appear to be depressed. It was his birthday, so he had a few drinks, not many, but he must have forgotten that he had already taken his medication."

Alan felt sorry for him. He was clearly in denial. It did not sound at all convincing, but clearly the subject was very raw for him. Could there have been a reason for his Ed to commit suicide, or was Richard capable of administering an overdose to him, and effectively killing him? So many questions without answers. He decided to change the subject.

"So what did you think about Stephen's whirlwind romance with Chloe, and what did you think of Chloe?"

166

Richard was pleased that the questioning had moved away from Ed. He was not sure he would ever get over the loss of Ed, who had been the love of his life, but now he had to make sure he gave the right answers to the next set of questions that were being put to him.

"Stephen lives in a romantic world, and this is reflected in his writing, so it was not too much of a surprise. I was happy to support Chloe with her mental welfare. She was a beautiful young lady, and clearly very attracted to Stephen. There was a vulnerability about her that made her very likeable."

"So you were happy about her marrying Stephen?"

"Why would I not be?"

Alan knew his next words would probably offend Richard immensely, but he had to know.

"You have known Stephen since you were at university together. Has your relationship ever been deeper than just friendship?"

Richard just hated the way this man was probing into his life, but he did not dare to lie to him because he had no idea what Stephen might say. Lying to the police was definitely not a good idea. He knew his face had reddened, and he had guilt written all over him. But inside he felt so angry!

"If you really must know, Stephen and I had a relationship when we were at university. It lasted for a year. Stephen was unsure of his sexuality at that time, and afterwards did have girlfriends. But after Ed and I became a couple, Stephen announced he was going to remain a bachelor, and then started his career of writing. These days we are just friends."

Alan was finding all this very interesting. Although Richard was being honest, it seemed that he was another possible suspect.

"Would you ever think about rekindling your relationship with Stephen?"

"No I would not. When we lived together I found he just had no idea how to control his money. He nearly made me bankrupt, that's why we parted. But I do have affection for him, and even now we are best friends."

Richard felt guilty about being disloyal to Stephen, but in a situation like this, he had to save himself. He felt that Clarke was looking for any reason to try and arrest him, and he felt really nervous.

"Thank you, Richard, you have been very helpful, and I do apologise for having to ask you such personal questions, but in a situation like this we have to get a clear picture," explained Alan.

"Natalie, you can stop recording now."

Richard Lyon saw them out of his office, and heaved a sigh of relief. It was incredible how that policeman had managed to get all that information out of him. His private life exposed; it felt as if it had all been stripped away.

He decided to phone Stephen and warn him that he had admitted to their past relationship, because if they questioned Stephen, and he denied it, then they would be all over them both like a rash. He just wanted to be left alone to lead his life, and he wanted privacy, but the police hanging around was definitely bad news.

Richard pressed the button to ring Stephen, and the phone only rang once before it was picked up: "Yes Richard."

"Stephen, I thought I had better warn you, that Detective Inspector Clarke has been round here questioning me again. It was awful. So many personal questions, asking if Ed committed suicide, and then he asked if you and I had ever had a relationship, so I had to tell him. I can't lie to anyone."

Stephen grimaced. He hadn't wanted the police to know about his gay period. Surely meeting and marrying Chloe last year was proof enough that he liked women.

"Richard, all I had wanted was a normal life and a family. I had no idea it was going to end like this."

Richard felt such empathy for him. Unbelievably, after all that had happened, he still had feelings for this man. He couldn't help worrying that Kay had let him down so badly, and now it might be hard to get another nanny. After all, Luke's mother had died. "Sorry to spring this on you, Stephen. I know you have your own problems. Have the agency managed to find you a new nanny?"

"No, it's such a worry, and like you said, I don't want to be too dependent on Anna. I think you are right, she has ideas in her head about us, and there is no us, I don't want her!"

Richard was surprised at the emotion in Stephen's words. But he still loved Chloe, it was early days, and of course he would feel like that.

168

"Well what are we going to do about a nanny?"

"I don't know, Richard. I was actually thinking about selling this house and maybe moving back to London, and then I might get another nanny."

Richard felt disappointment sweep through him. No more games of tennis in Ramsgate, or golf, no more trips to the beach, it was an entirely different life in London, and he would not see Stephen so often. He felt that overwhelming feeling of loneliness sweep over him again.

"I thought you liked life in Broadstairs," he said, sadly.

"Oh, I do. I have a perfect study where I can contemplate and write. The house is full of character, and as you know it's a few minutes walk to the shops and the beach. But I find Anna stifling, I need her to go, and I can't manage Luke on my own. Unlike you, I know nothing about babies."

"Well, he is over four months now, I think it's time you learned! How about I move in for a bit, and we share caring for him together. At least with your job, you can do it anywhere that you live."

Stephen was about to scoff at him, and tell him he just wasn't into babies, but he knew Richard would not let him get away with that. Nowadays there were house husbands when the wife went out to work, and even male nannies. The idea of Richard moving in and showing him how to care for Luke really did appeal to him. Richard had always proved to be his best friend. Having him in the house would make it feel much brighter, and he could finally get rid of clinging Anna.

"Richard, I would love that," he said, feeling very relieved.

"It's not going to be permanent, just to help a friend in need for a while," Richard reminded him.

"Of course, I will tell Anna tomorrow that we don't need her any more."

Just at that moment, the doorbell went, and when Stephen looked out of the window he recognised the police car. He could hear Anna going to answer the door, and he held his breath for a second before speaking again.

"Oh no, Richard, they have come to question me now, but at least I know what to say."

169

h

"OK, ring me later," said Richard, and Stephen hastily clicked his mobile off, and then waited with trepidation for Anna to tell him that the police wanted to talk to him. He could hear their voices below him and the sound of the kettle boiling, and he realised they were here to interview Anna. Breathing a sigh of relief, he retreated back into his study, which was his safe haven, and quietly sat down at his desk.

Alan went back to his office after the interview with Richard. He was hoping James had managed to see Monique, and find out whether his hunch about her knowing Kay was right. When he arrived, James and Martha had finished their lunch, and Martha had typed up the interview with Monique so he could read it.

He had stopped off at a Marks and Spencer Food Hall to get himself a sandwich, and Martha got him some coffee to drink whilst he was munching it. He quickly scanned the paperwork, and then turned his attention to James.

"How did it go with Monique today? I hope she didn't react too emotionally."

"No sir, the nurse made it clear we could not have long with her, and she was very co-operative. You were absolutely correct, she does know Kay, and they did both provide each other with references for their jobs. Of course, I made it clear it was illegal, but she already knew that. She explained that she had been sacked from her previous job, and was desperate. I did not get into the subject of why, because that is a separate case altogether, and leads us away from the murder enquiry."

Alan nodded his head. "Monique lived in a flat at Ramsgate before she joined us, I presume that is how they knew each other."

"Yes, in fact the same block, but what is most interesting is the fact that she still lived there on 24th May, as she joined you on 28th, so naturally I asked her for an alibi for the evening of 24th. She said that after hearing that she had got the job working for you and Zoe, on that evening herself and Kay went for a walk around the Ramsgate Harbour area, ending up at a little snack bar at the top overlooking the beach and harbour. They got home about ten o'clock, just as it was getting dark. The statement that you took from Kay clearly stated that after she finished work, she went back to her flat and was in all night."

"So she lied!" exclaimed Alan. She was another one he could not trust.

"Yes, now seeing as Chloe was killed after ten o'clock, it would have been possible for either of them to get back to Broadstairs, but buses at that time of night are few and far between. I asked Monique if she knew Chloe, she said she had never met her."

"What about Stephen, does she know him?"

"I did not ask that. Sorry sir."

"It's OK James, it sounds like you have done very well. I am over there after lunch, interviewing Anna, I can ask him then."

"That's good."

"In fact, James, something you said earlier at our team briefing has given me food for thought since I interviewed Richard Lyon. When I mentioned he was gay, you made a joke about him being secretly in love with Stephen, and murdering Chloe so he could move in with him. That may not be too far from the truth."

Martha had been listening intently to all this, and her face took on an expression of surprise.

"Wow, this investigation seems to be full of surprises. I never even thought about Richard."

"Well there is no time to explain it all now, but at the briefing tomorrow it will all be discussed. If James is happy to let you go, you can come with me to interview Anna. We have an appointment at two-thirty."

"Of course," said James. "Where is Natalie?"

"Natalie is getting our interview with Richard Lyon typed up. That interview is full of surprises," said Alan, very cryptically. "She took her sandwich along to your office so she could do both things at once. I told her to have a break, but she wanted to do it."

James smiled to himself. Natalie would have wanted to impress Alan with her efficiency, and she had certainly done that.

Alan screwed up the empty sandwich packet and threw it in the bin, he then glanced at his watch. "OK, if you are ready Martha, we need to head over to Broadstairs to interview Anna. It's easily a half hour drive."

Martha had been expecting Alan to want to leave the moment he was finished. When he was deep in a murder case, everything else was pushed aside. Luckily she had eaten before he arrived back, and had time to go and renew her lipstick and freshen up before they did the next interview. This was something Alan just would not understand. He was single-minded, and totally focused on his job.

She rose from her chair, and James took himself back to his own office, where Natalie was still typing up the report. Alan had said it would be a revelation, so that had really aroused his curiosity. It would be interesting to bandy around everyone's different theories at the briefing tomorrow.

Alan and Martha got into the car. As usual he had to drive slowly through Canterbury, as it was always busy, and just to add to their difficulties there were temporary traffic lights at the top of Burgate. Alan was tapping his fingers impatiently on the wheel, anxious to get going as quickly as possible.

When they reached Sturry, the level crossing was open, so they did not have to queue up there, then he turned right and proceeded along the main road towards Thanet that took him past Upstreet and Grove Ferry. Traffic was lighter there, so he was able to make up a bit of time. By the time they passed Westwood Cross Shopping Centre it was twenty past two, so hopefully they would be at Stone Road within the next few minutes. Alan had always been a stickler for punctuality, and he never liked to be late anywhere, even if there was a good reason for it.

He parked the car outside the house, and noticed a face at the window upstairs which appeared to be Stephen Ward. He had expected him to be in, as the man never seemed to go far from his house, so he could speak to him a bit later. Right now it was Anna they wanted to speak to. After ringing the doorbell, they waited patiently until she opened the door. She had a papoose strapped to her body, and inside baby Luke was fast asleep. She smiled pleasantly at them both, and privately Martha was thinking she looked like Mother Earth. She wondered why Anna had the baby strapped to her whilst she was around the house, it must make her chores much harder to do. Didn't he have a cot to sleep in?

"Good afternoon," said Alan, politely. He didn't know Anna that well. They had met her twice. Once when she came into the police station and then at the funeral. Up until now, she had not even been considered as a suspect, but this investigation had so many different angles to view it from. "I hope we haven't stopped you from going out."

Anna beamed. "Not at all, we just got back from the shops. I am glad we made it in time. If you can give me five minutes, I will transfer Luke to his cot, and let Stephen know we are back. In the meantime, I will also put the kettle on."

"Of course," murmured Alan. This woman was like a mini tornado, rushing about. She quickly opened the door to the lounge, and they both sat down on the sofa. Then they first heard her in the kitchen with the kettle, and then heard her mounting the stairs, presumably to let Stephen know they were there, Alan thought.

Having decided the visit was not to him, Stephen had retired to his study. He felt this was the place where all the magic happened. He was halfway through a romantic story, which encompassed a similar situation to his own life, when he met Chloe. He felt it was a fitting tribute to her, and when it was published, he had no doubt his fans would love it. Although his story would have a happy ending, nothing other than happiness was allowed in his romantic tales.

He heard Anna's footsteps on the stairs. It had been so nice and quiet whilst she was out, and now the police had arrived and it looked like she was coming to announce they were here. Anna's personality absolutely overwhelmed him. She always appeared to be so attention seeking, and he wondered how Chloe had managed to endure her friendship for all of her life, or had she just put up with her, because Chloe was so good natured. When Chloe had been alive, he had seen Anna a few times, and always got the impression that she didn't approve of him. She seemed to be jealous that, with him around, Chloe was no longer so available, and she didn't like it.

But since Chloe had passed on, Anna had clung to him like a limpet, and it had not taken him long to realise that Richard was right, she was doing everything she could to make him notice her, and make herself completely indispensable by taking charge of Luke. But then, he remembered, Richard was going to save the day. He wished he had not told her about Ed's suicide. At the time he had thought he could trust her, but now he was not so sure. He also wondered if Anna was behind Kay's swift departure, which angered him, as it has left them in a right mess.

Unaware of Stephen's thoughts about her, Anna popped her head through the door. She smiled at him, and he noticed she was wearing a blue dress that had previously belonged to Chloe, and also she had coloured her hair to the same auburn shade as Chloe's, as well as changing her hair style to a full fringe worn long and straight in a direct imitation of Chloe. This woman made him sick!

"Hi Stephen, we are back now, and I have put Luke down for his nap. Alan Clarke is here. He wants to interview me. Do you want to come down and join us?"

Stephen stared at her in disbelief. She actually sounded like this was her house. She was a hostess inviting him to take part in a charade that involved being questioned about a murder enquiry. He wanted to keep as far away as possible, not only from Anna, but the police as well. He just wanted to be left alone in his house to quietly get on with his writing, and his thoughts. He thought it was about time he let her know she was going. But he would be polite about it, so she didn't have any reason to say anything bad about him. He knew his manners.

"Anna, I am so grateful for the way you stepped in to help me out when Kay left."

"That's OK," she beamed at him.

"Just to let you know that you can now pick up your own job again, as you won't be needed any more."

Anna stared at him, totally aghast. For once in her life she was rendered speechless. She had found that, since Chloe was not around, her feelings for Stephen had changed. He was a public figure, and he didn't leave the house too much, but when he did people came up to him for an autograph, and told him how much they loved his books. He was also a very handsome man. He kept himself fit with all the golf and tennis that he played. She had been so proud to be working alongside him. She had even been prepared to be Luke's stepmother when he asked her to marry him, because she was sure he would. She was sure that Stephen loved her as much as she loved him, and if Chloe was up there somewhere looking down she would be delighted that he had married her best friend.

But she was now realising in that moment that although this was her dream, and her fantasy, it was not his. He actually wanted her to go. She would not be needed again, and at that very moment her love turned to hate! He had made a fool of her, and she owed this man no loyalty whatsoever. She had never been good at keeping secrets, but she had kept Chloe's secret about Luke for the last year, but now she didn't care who knew it. She had previously confided to the police because she had believed that maybe the man from the fairground had killed Chloe, and she didn't want him to get away with it. But now she felt so angry, she was happy to blacken Stephen's name, just to make herself feel better.

She kept her voice controlled, but her eyes glittered with barely suppressed rage.

"So you have a new nanny, then. The agency found one?"

"Oh no, it's not that easy, because not many want to come into the house where there has been a death. Richard is coming to stay for a while, and we are going to share the chores together."

She wanted to shout and scream at him. So he was having his gay friend to come and live there; now that definitely sounded suspicious, but if by any chance Stephen was bisexual, Richard was a person she could not compete with, and it was eating her up inside.

The anger inside her made her want to shout and scream at him for leading her astray, because that is what it felt like, and then she could storm out of the house, and he would be left with the very embarrassing task of placating the police. But then she thought of a better way to blacken his name.

She could talk to the police about him and drag his name through the mud; that would be much more satisfying. "I hope you will both be very happy together," she said, in a sarcastic voice. She couldn't help it, that man had ruined her life. "When do you want me to go?"

Stephen smiled pleasantly at her, even though he was feeling angry inside. He had noticed the sarcasm in her tone, and she had implied that when Richard came, they would be a couple. She was just a troublemaker, and he needed her out of this house right now. "Richard is moving in tomorrow, but I want to give you some financial compensation for helping me out when I needed it."

He had hoped that money might soften the blow, but her next words proved this to be wrong.

"I won't come in tomorrow then, and you can keep your money. I didn't do it for money, I did it for you."

Her words had no effect on him, so she turned on her heel and left the room. It was all she could do not to bang the door shut. She went quickly down the stairs, and then entered the kitchen and made two cups of coffee. She carried the full cups into the front room, where Alan and Martha were sitting.

She had been upstairs no more than five minutes, but Alan could see that whatever had been said to her had completely changed her demeanour. The sparkle in her eyes had gone and she appeared to be seething with anger; this was definitely not a happy house.

Chapter Twenty-six

"Thank you for seeing us this afternoon, Anna. There are a few things we need to clear up with you," Alan said briskly. She looked as if she had a right mood on her, so he wanted to get this done as soon as possible.

"I hope I can be of use to you," said Anna. It was a good thing he couldn't see the anger and feeling of rejection inside her. She sincerely hoped he would ask her something that would drop Stephen Ward right in it!

"I want to take you back to May of 2023, when Chloe's father died suddenly. As you stated, you have been Chloe's closest friend since you were young children at school together. I was wondering why you were not around, not only when he passed away so tragically, but also to give support to Chloe at the funeral?"

"If you only knew how much I wish I had been. My parents had been saving up to go on a cruise, and we went away a couple of days before Norman passed away, and we were away for a month. When we came back, the funeral had already taken place. Apparently Chloe had tried to contact me on the ship, but if you know anything about the signal when you are in the middle of nowhere, then you will understand. I often think if I had been around to support her at the funeral, she may not have got herself pregnant.

"Well, as there has not been a DNA test done, it's possible that Luke may be Stephen's son anyway," said Alan, as pleasantly as he could. Her attitude was entirely that she was really hoping Stephen wasn't Luke's father.

"Certainly, he is bringing him up as if he was," said Anna, making a mental note to tell Stephen there was a doubt about Luke's parentage.

"Next question concerns the evening of 24th May," continued Alan, determined not to stray off topic.

"The night Chloe was murdered," echoed Anna.

"Yes, correct. Can you let me know your movements that evening?"

"Yes, it was the night before bank holiday Saturday. It was a lovely sunny evening, and my dad did a barbecue in the garden. He cooks a mean steak."

"Presumably this barbecue lasted until it got dark. What did you do after that?"

"We just went inside and cleared up, then we watched TV until bedtime."

"So your parents will confirm this."

"Of course they will," said Anna. Her bedtime was always around ten-thirty, after news at ten. But she would never forget that night, because she had crept out of the house without her parents knowing, and she did not want this nosey policeman to know. One of the workers at the fair had sent her a text asking to meet her up by the funfair. It was Vincent's cousin Ned, and she knew there was no way her parents would have approved of her doing that.

She felt as she wasn't a teenager any more, she could please herself. Anna had always had trouble keeping a boyfriend, and there was a certain ruggedness about the travellers that attracted her. Although there was no way she was going to make the same mistake as Chloe had and get herself pregnant. Her parents had gone to bed themselves at ten-thirty as well, and by quarter to eleven all was quiet. She had slipped out the back door, and driven her car up the road to the promenade where the fair was set up. She had arrived there within a couple of minutes, but Ned had not turned up. She felt angry and humiliated, so had told no one, and quietly driven herself back home and gone back to bed.

Anna was so confident of herself, she wrote her mother's mobile number on a piece of paper, and told Alan if he rang her, she would confirm Anna's account of that evening.

"OK, thanks, I will do that later," said Alan, handing the piece of paper to Martha, who put it securely in the case with her mobile phone.

"How did you get on with Kay?" asked Alan.

"Kay was OK. At least I thought so until she went without telling anyone."

She could have added that she had not liked the familiarity Kay showed towards Stephen, nor the way that she seemed to be trying to get her feet under the table. But that sounded as if she was jealous, and, of course, she was, but there was no need for Alan Clarke to know that. She had been glad to see the back of Kay Wilson, but it hardly mattered now, because she was being dumped, and for who, his gay best friend! What an insult!

Although she was answering his questions, there was an attitude about her as though someone had ruffled her feathers. Martha had noticed it too. He wondered if Anna had had some sort of argument with Stephen.

"How do you find Stephen?"

"What do you mean?" she asked, feeling puzzled.

"Well, if you cast your mind back to when we interviewed you before, you said that Chloe had changed since she married Stephen, and that you felt he was coercively controlling her. You were concerned that he had forced her to give up her business."

"Yes, I did think all that about him. When Chloe died he inherited this house, and her business, which apparently he has now sold. But she's not here to control now, is she? Mark my words, he has done very well financially from her death."

Alan knew exactly what she was implying. Obviously her boss had done something to upset her today, as she was showing absolutely no loyalty towards him.

"But then you came to the station and told us you had misjudged him, and he was sensitive and kind. You can't have it both ways, Anna. Either he is a good boss or he is not, according to what sort of mood you are in that day, it seems to me!"

Alan was very annoyed. How could they believe a word she said?

179

People like her, who blew hot and cold, were completely unreliable as any sort of witness.

Anna looked defiantly at him. "If you remember he let me help him plan Chloe's funeral, and at that time I felt close to him because we both loved her, but he has changed recently."

"So in what way has he changed?" Alan glanced over at Martha, who was keeping out of this one, and he wondered what sort of nonsense Anna would come out with next.

"Since Chloe died, he has shut himself in his study. He says he is writing, but he plays no part in Luke's welfare, and never changes a nappy or feeds him."

"But generally that has been your job, hasn't it?"

"Well that is what I thought, but just now Stephen informed me that I am no longer required, because his best friend Richard, who we all know is gay, is moving into here to help him with Luke. Apparently the agency cannot find him a nanny, because nobody wants to come and work in a house where a mother was murdered."

Now Alan could see why her mood had changed. Stephen must have told her about Richard coming to stay when they first arrived, and she had popped upstairs to let him know that she was back and they were here. Of course, she was trying to imply that they were having a gay relationship because that made her feel better about the fact that she was no longer required.

But although she was being quite a drama queen, Alan was privately wondering if they were having a gay relationship. If they were, then Richard moving in would be significant, and it would also make him a suspect, as with Chloe now passed on, and a house he could live in at Broadstairs, Richard would have had a motive to kill Chloe.

He once again changed the subject. "Do you know who Monique Duval is?"

Anna looked blankly at him. If she was acting, she was doing it well.

"The name means nothing to me. Should it?"

"Not really," muttered Alan. He did not want her to know it was his ex-nanny. Up until now, it seemed that only Kay had known Monique, and had never spoken about her. Now that Monique had left employment with him, maybe it would not be considered to be too close to home. What he really needed was for someone to tell him that Monique had not been at Broadstairs that evening so he could eliminate her from the enquiry. But as long as no one could prove her innocence, she remained the reason that he might have to pass the case onto someone else, and he did not want to do that, he wanted to see it through and get justice for Chloe.

"Thank you, Anna, for helping us. I just want to speak to Stephen before we go, and then we are done," said Alan, trying to sound genial. Something about Anna got right under his skin. She was not likeable, and yet she had been Chloe's best friend for all those years. Chloe must have trusted her to tell her about the one night stand with Vince.

Anna felt so relieved. Thank goodness her parents had not heard her come and go on that evening of 24th May. Without a doubt her mother would say that Anna had remained with them all evening, and then went to bed at ten-thirty. She walked towards the door.

"I will let Stephen know you wish to speak to him now, and if you will excuse me, I need to go and check on Luke."

She left the room in rather dramatic fashion, as seemed to be her way, sweeping through the door and then closing it quite firmly. Alan and Martha exchanged glances. He raised his eyebrows at her without speaking, conscious of the fact that they were not in a safe environment, and this house might well have something set up to record what they said unofficially to each other. Maybe he was getting over dramatic, but he preferred to discuss his analysis either in the car, or at the safety of the police station.

About five minutes later, Stephen Ward entered the room. He had the same anxious look that Alan had noticed before. He was dressed casually in shorts and tee shirt, as if he was on his way to the beach, but Anna had said he spent most of his time shut in his office. It seemed like when he did go out, it was to play tennis, or golf with Richard, and he did belong to a gym. There had been no mention of him having any friends other than Richard, so it did sound as though he was a bit of a hermit.

"Good afternoon, officer. What can I do for you?" he asked, feeling anxious because he had no idea what Anna had told Alan, but he felt pretty sure she would have mentioned the fact that Richard was moving in to help with Luke, because he had seen how annoyed she was about this, and he also sensed she wanted to cause as much trouble as she could now that she was leaving. The phrase 'hell hath no fury' certainly had a meaning here, but it had been necessary to get rid of her now, not just because Richard was coming, but because she wanted to become a couple with him, and he most certainly did not want that.

"We are sorry to disturb you, Stephen, I just wondered if you knew a lady called Monique Duval?"

Stephen also gave him a blank look. "I don't think so. The only friend of Chloe that I knew about was Anna."

Alan didn't feel as though he needed to explain who she was. His nanny situation was nothing to do with anyone else. Each time someone was questioned, it appeared that Monique and Kay had kept their friendship a secret. Probably because they had falsified each other's references.

"Well, thanks very much," said Alan, cheerfully. He was pleased to be getting out of here. He nodded at Martha to stop recording.

When they were driving back to Canterbury, he noticed the clock in the car was showing three-thirty, he hoped he could get away on time today, as not only was it Zoe's first full day without a nanny to help her, but also he had to explain about James interviewing Monique, because as it was so soon after her breakdown, Zoe might not be too pleased to hear about it. But hopefully when he explained she would.

"What did you make of Anna then? He asked, diverting himself back to the present.

Martha screwed up her face. "Not very much, actually. She changes her opinions as often as her clothes, and she has no loyalty to her boss."

"I totally agree, and yet she was Chloe's closest friend."

"She said that, remember. Chloe is not here to confirm or deny it."

Alan was thoughtful. "You have a point there, but don't forget, Chloe did entrust her with her most personal secret. If Vince had denied it, I would have believed him and thought that she was lying, but when I jumped on him, he did admit it."

"I wonder how Stephen would react if he knew that?"

"Now that she has been dispensed with, I wouldn't put anything past her, so watch this space!" said Alan, grimacing. Some women were such difficult creatures, and Anna was one of them.

They had reached Canterbury Police station now, so Alan parked the car and went inside. He had plenty of notes to look through before the briefing tomorrow. Martha went to get the recorded interview with Anna, and Stephen's denial of knowing Monique, typed up. She preferred to work alone in another room, and then bring the results back to Alan.

Alan read through it all carefully. It was a good thing it was all recorded first, as it was really difficult to remember every little detail. There were at least three people who could have been the murderer, and there was so little evidence, in fact no evidence, and nobody really had safe alibis. He was aware that Vince's girlfriend Lena could have come looking for him that night, and Richard admitted to driving around Broadstairs looking for Chloe, as for Monique and Kay, they could have got a taxi back to Broadstairs. He could just go on like this, but right now he needed to rest his brain, he needed to get back to his lovely wife and home environment, which was so different from the world of crimes that he tried to solve.

Martha came back into the office. "Yes, that is all done, ready for tomorrow. Oh, and by the way, I have spoken to Anna's mother, and she confirmed her movements on 24th May."

"Of course she did. But how are we to know if she waited for her parents to go to bed, and then crept out of the house? She wouldn't be the first person to do that."

"Agreed, I did it a couple of times when I was a teenager, but proving it's another thing," said Martha, handing him the paperwork, and Alan added it to the rest of the folder.

"OK Martha, it's now four-thirty, too late to start on anything else, and we both have homes to go to."

"Well actually I have some shopping to get. Our fridge is looking pretty empty. I think I will be finished shopping about the time that Clive finishes his shift, so if I can go now boss, that would work well."

"Yes, off you go Martha. Can't have your man going hungry."
Alan smiled. Clive was a well built man who clearly loved his food.
"Thanks very much for today. We can start the debrief at ten o'clock,
and I want everyone there, participation will be very important."

"Yes, I will see to that. Good night, sir, and thanks so much," said
Martha, collecting her handbag which was hanging from the chair,
then she picked up her mobile phone and was gone.

Chapter Twenty-seven

Zoe had just spent her first day since Erica had been born without any help from anyone, and she had managed to cope with her two little ones. It had given her a newly found confidence. That terrible crushing feeling of defeat and numbness had gone, and her naturally bubbly nature was returning.

She had been worried about how she would cope, but apart from feeling tired, which was normal, she had felt she was in control. Her natural motherly feelings towards Erica were there, and that feeling that she would keep her safe from anything was there too. The indifference had gone, and she knew that, in a way, Monique had helped with that. When she had seen her, possessively clutching Erica close to her, it had roused feelings of jealousy because Erica was her baby, and then when Monique brandished the knife, and she thought her baby was in danger, inside her, as well as fear, was rage. She was a lioness protecting her cub, and at that moment, she realised just how precious her baby daughter was.

Since then she had time to reflect on the events, and all she could feel for Monique was sadness. The poor girl had never been loved, no father, and a dysfunctional mother. What chance had she stood in life? No wonder she had suffered a breakdown.

Zoe had compared her life to Monique's. She had come from a loving home, with support and guidance from her family, and now she had the love of a good man, and two beautiful children. A little while ago, she had felt numb, but right now she felt awake again, and it was such a relief. She felt ready to assume the reins of motherhood, and this was because she realised that, no matter how bad she had thought her predicament was, she only had to look around herself and see someone who was much worse off, namely Monique, and therefore be grateful for all she had.

She was very happy when she got the text from Alan to say he would be home by five o'clock, and he hoped everything was OK. She was looking forward to spending the evening with him. Just the two of them, it had been a while since that happened. She picked up her phone to text back.

She had found some steak in the freezer. It had been defrosting all day, and was one of Alan's favourite meals. He liked it cooked with mushrooms and oven chips, so it didn't take long to prepare. Adam was in his high chair eating spaghetti bolognese, which was one of his favourite meals, and Erica was lying peacefully on her baby rug having a little kick.

She looked over at her, and Erica rewarded her mother with a cheesy smile, which captured Zoe's heart. She picked her up from the floor and gave her a kiss on her soft little cheek. Then putting her gently back, she said, "You are Mummy's lovely little girl."

"Mummy, me finish," said Adam from the depths of his high chair, well aware that his mother's attention was elsewhere. Right now his sister was a tiny doll that cried, to him, he was too young to understand that she was real.

When Zoe went over to him, he turned his face towards her, and it was orange. The pasta sauce was orange, and it was in his hair, round his eyes and mouth, and his fingers were also covered in it, because he had used them more than his spoon to get the pasta into his mouth. Whereas a little while ago, Zoe would have been in despair to see all the mess, today she could see the funny side of it. She giggled, and with one swift movement she lifted him out of his high chair.

Then she remembered Erica on the floor, so she quickly put her into her baby chair, and made sure she was strapped in. Then she picked up Adam and took him to the bathroom. She undressed him whilst the bath was filling with water, then added some bubble bath. Having checked that it was both warm enough and full enough, she lifted him into the bath, and then added the toys he loved to play with in there.

"Mummy will be back in a minute," she told him as she quickly went downstairs intending to bring Erica up too. Her baby daughter was asleep, so she took her out of the chair, and put her into her cot. Laying her carefully on her side. Then she went back into the bathroom. Now she could give Adam her undivided attention, so she knelt by the bath pretending to steal his duck. He was squealing with laughter, and whilst he was playing she was using the sponge with soapy water to try and wash off the offending orange pasta sauce. Then she heard the front door opening.

"I am home. Where is everybody?"

Adam crowed with delight to hear his father's voice, and Zoe called out.

"We're upstairs in the bathroom."

Alan took the stairs two at a time. He couldn't wait to see them all, his precious family. He bent down to where Zoe was kneeling, and hugged and kissed her. "Hi honey, how has it been today?"

"Good," beamed Zoe. "I am learning to be a mother again."

"You have always been that," he assured her. It was amazing to see her sparkle back. That anxious look in here eyes had gone, but he still had to tell her about Monique.

He went to the airing cupboard and got out Adam's hooded towel. "What a clean boy you are. Daddy is going to dry you, then Mummy can take a break."

"You would not have said that if you saw him ten minutes ago. He had turned orange, as he was completely covered in pasta sauce," said Zoe, laughing mischievously. Alan was delighted to see her like that. He had now got his real Zoe back.

After Alan had dried and dressed Adam ready for bed, he was put back into his high chair to watch a bit of TV before his bedtime. Erica had now woken up, and it was her turn to be fed and then prepared for bed. Alan could see it was a different Zoe who was caring for her now. She confidently handled her, and it wasn't long before she too was ready for bed. He went out into the kitchen to see if Zoe needed any help with vegetables, and his eyes lit up when he saw the steak in the fridge. She had washed the mushrooms, and chopped them smaller, and even the oven chips had been moved to the front of the freezer for easy access when needed.

"Well you are well organised tonight," he said. "Zoe, I am so proud of you, not many women could have seen off the curse of post natal depression the way you have."

Zoe blushed. "I knew the help was there, and I was loved, unlike poor Monique, so it gave me the push I needed to fight back."

"Can I have a cuddle with my daughter now?" asked Alan, gathering her up from the rug where she was kicking her legs enthusiastically and gurgling. He didn't want to talk about Monique yet, it was too complicated, and he planned to wait until both the babes were in bed, and they were alone.

"Why not, she is so easy to spoil," agreed Zoe. Erica was already making eye contact and smiling. Alan was totally entranced with her when he saw her smile. He was so proud of both of his children.

Later, when they sat down after eating their steak washed down with a bottle of red wine, Alan was feeling relaxed and contented. Now he was going to discuss Monique.

"Did you contact the hospital today? I just wondered how Monique was doing."

Zoe glanced at him in surprise. She had not been sure whether Alan shared her empathy towards Monique, as he had not said much yesterday. "I did ring up, and she had a good night's sleep, and they suggested I waited a few more days before visiting so they can have a clearer picture of her needs."

Alan cleared his throat. "As you know, I am duty bound to not share information about my case with anyone outside the police station. We have been here before, but like last time, certain aspects of the case have collided with our private life, and so now I have to share a few things with you, and I need to explain why."

Zoe looked totally mystified. Alan was beating around the bush, and she needed to know what he wanted to tell her. "You know it will go no further than me."

"Of course, honey, I do. It's quite complicated, but as you know this case has not been solved yet. Tomorrow we have a team briefing, which sometimes helps, as colleagues can sometimes spot things that I might have missed."

"Go on, then."

"When I went to Yorkshire, it was to interview the ex-nanny of Stephen Ward. She left without word under suspicious circumstances. We had to be sure she was safe, so I went there to check."

"Was she safe?"

"Yes, she had moved back home with her parents. During our conversation, she admitted that she had forged her references."

"The same as Monique," interjected Zoe, remembering what Monique had told her.

"Yes, when you told me, it seemed odd that they both said they had done that, so then I wondered if the two nannies actually knew each other." He paused, knowing the next part might not please Zoe.

"I had to mention it in my report, and it immediately became clear that Monique needed to be interviewed ASAP. It also appeared to be a conflict of interest, so I had to send another officer to interview her."

"Has she been interviewed?"

"She has, and I was right, they are friends and both falsified references for each other."

"So she was interviewed today then?"

"This morning, in fact. I am now hoping that, as Monique no longer works for us, I can continue with the investigation. I want to get justice for Chloe and her son Luke."

Alan had been expecting Zoe to chide him for allowing anyone to interview Monique so soon after she had been admitted to hospital, but she leaned her head against his shoulder, and snuggled nearer to him on the sofa.

"I am so proud of you, Alan," she said, feeling very emotional. "You don't need to worry any more about Monique. She is in the best place to help her. I will keep in touch with her, of course, but we both know she will never come back here to work. She did care for our babes admirably, no complaints there, but I can manage now, and when my maternity leave finishes next year, Helen will be back. If Monique has done something wrong, hopefully she is in the right place to get the help that she needs."

"Personally I don't think she has. It's just her association with the other nanny has given us a bit of a headache, but it's not for us to worry about, and the sooner I can get to the truth the better."

189

"Of course, if I had known how emotionally unstable the poor girl was, she wouldn't have come here to work, but we both liked the fact that Adam loved her."

"Honey, you can't blame yourself, I was the one who advertised online because the agency had nothing to offer us at that time, but looking back we both know our mistake. We should have contacted the couple at the address on the reference, and then we would have known they were fake."

"Yes, our children are so precious. Next time we will be more vigilant," said Zoe. "We will never make that mistake again."

Chapter Twenty-eight

Alan was up early the next day, anxious to get on with the team briefing. He had read through all the statements so many times and realised that where Kay Wilson was concerned, she needed to be interviewed again, but he didn't fancy travelling back to Yorkshire simply to ask her why she had lied about her alibi. Her statement clearly said she had finished at five o'clock, then gone home to her flat at Ramsgate, and then she had stayed in all evening.

Then an idea struck him. Maybe he could get Martha to contact her and set up a Zoom meeting, then, if he still felt dissatisfied with her answers, a car would be sent to bring her to Canterbury for more questioning. He decided to mention it at the briefing. Although, if he was honest with himself, he was not happy about most of their alibis; none of them seemed safe.

He didn't get involved with the children this morning, other than to give them both a kiss and say that he loved them. Sometimes he helped to feed Adam, or dress him, or even give Erica her bottle, but today his priority had to be to get to work, and then involve his colleagues in the team briefing. The case seemed to be dragging on with no satisfactory conclusion.

Zoe understood completely. She knew how driven Alan was. His aim was to get this case solved and arrest the culprit so that Broadstairs would go back to being the safe seaside town that many people liked to visit. It only took one person to destroy an area with such an evil act, and then people would not go there and local

191

businesses would suffer, so he would be very keen to find the culprit.

He left home a little earlier than usual, but not before he had been assured by Zoe that she was now feeling much better. "I hope to be home normal time honey, but if I am going to be late, I will let you know."

Zoe returned his hug, and wished him a great day. Then she picked up Adam so he could reach his dad. Adam had just learned to shake hands, so Alan was treated to that before he left the house. He couldn't help smiling to himself in the car; Adam was such a star, in fact, his whole family were, especially Zoe. He was married to the girl of his dreams, and he wondered how he had been so lucky, because he reckoned being married to him could not be easy. All those call outs just as he was about to spend time with his family, and cancelled events, but Zoe had always taken it all in her stride, and frequently told him she wouldn't want him to be any other way.

He arrived at the station earlier than usual, and, to his surprise, Martha was also there early. She had already gone into the room where the debrief was going to take place, and pinned up photos of all the suspects with anything that stood out written in marker pen. He paused by the photo of Chloe in her familiar white neck scarf. She looked so happy, and beautiful, so it must have been taken before she started suffering from mental health problems.

Alan returned to his own office. Martha had the folder on the desk with all the typed out interviews inside, and he glanced through it all to familiarise himself before he addressed the meeting. There were so many of them. Usually murder cases had up to four suspects, but this one felt like many more.

Martha came bustling in with coffee, which Alan was pleased to see. "I must thank you, Martha, for coming in early and organising everything for me. I see you have also pinned all the photos up in the room where we are meeting."

"You are welcome, sir," Martha beamed, and then they both sat there in companionable silence, sipping their coffees.

By the time ten o'clock came, Alan felt as if he had been at work for hours. When he entered the room with Martha, he was thankful to see a gathering of about ten other police officers, with a good mix of men and women, which pleased him, as he liked to hear the opinions of both sexes.

He strode over to the board and, using a ruler, he pointed at the photo of Chloe.

"Good morning, ladies and gentleman, thank you very much for joining me this morning for this debrief. I value the opinion of every single one of you, so if you have an opinion, don't forget to speak up."

There was a murmur from everyone gathered there, and they all looked at each other. They knew that the way to get on was to spot something the boss might have missed and impress him with it.

Alan continued, "This is Chloe Ward, a young lady of twenty-three who was murdered. She was strangled with her own scarf and the post-mortem showed traces of heroin in her blood. What we know about her is she was a successful business woman, with her own shop, and lived alone with her father until he unexpectedly passed away in 2023. After this her life seemed to go awry. She suffered from mental health problems, and after a one night stand with a gypsy from the funfair, she went away to Crete for a holiday, where she met Stephen Ward and he married her shortly after. Her son Luke was born in February this year, and apparently she told her friend Anna that she didn't know which man was his father. Also she was being treated for her mental health problems by Richard Lyon, a close friend of her husband.

"Is that not a conflict of interest, sir?" queried James, and there was a murmur of agreement from the others.

"We did query that with Stephen Ward, but he seemed to think it was OK," Alan replied.

"Maybe we should all note that down," suggested Martha, and there was a rustle as pens were put to paper.

"Now I am moving on to Stephen Ward, husband of the deceased," said Alan, pointing towards the picture of him. "Out of all the suspects, he stood to gain the most from her death. He was declared bankrupt before he met her, and when they got married he moved into her Broadstairs home. Obviously he inherited her home and her business when she died. And is now currently living there with her baby son."

j

"Is that Stephen Ward the writer?" asked Leanne Ross, a young WPC.

"Correct," said Alan.

"I have read some of his books. They are full of warmth and happiness, which we all need more of," she said.

"Yes, it's called looking at the world through rose coloured glasses," said Martha, who had not been impressed by Stephen. "I think he lived in a dream world, and he was so busy being in there, he was unable to help his wife with her mental health problems. After all, let's face it, with their combined looks, talent and money, they should have been the happiest couple alive."

"Maybe that's a bit harsh," argued back Leanne. "There are often many reasons for mental health problems."

"Thank you Ladies, for your opinions. Now we have to press on," said Alan.

"Next up we have Sam Turner, a young lad of eighteen, who is on the autistic spectrum. When the police officers found Chloe's body, he was sitting next to her on the bench trying to untie her scarf."

"Sounds like he was caught in the act," said another voice.

"Yes is does, but often it's not the most obvious person. Having interviewed Sam and his mother, I am not convinced," said Alan.

"This next person is Richard Lyon, best friend of Stephen, and Chloe's psychologist. He is gay and aged thirty-four. His long term partner of ten years died of a prescription drug overdose two years ago. When interviewed he admitted that he had once had a relationship with Stephen for a year. He has now moved into the house to help care for the baby since the nanny left. I think he is the most likely person to have killed Chloe."

"Why is that, sir?" asked James, standing up.

"With Chloe gone, he gets to rekindle his relationship with Stephen, who appears to be bisexual."

James nodded and returned to his seat.

Alan pointed at the picture of Vince Mulligan.

"This is Vince Mulligan, aged twenty-seven, and a traveller from a local fair. He was originally our main suspect. He may be Luke's father, and he smokes pot. But he continually denied taking heroin. I haven't been able to prove that he did."

"Surely Dr Richard Lyon would have more access to heroin than any of the others?" said James.

"James, this is what I think," said Alan thoughtfully. "Another point is that heroin is very expensive to buy, and Richard is a wealthy man, whereas the others are just ordinary people."

He realised as he was speaking, the finger was being very firmly pointed in the direction of Richard.

"Gypsies are always well off, and they deal in cash, don't rule out Vince Mulligan," pointed out Natalie. She had been with Alan when he interviewed Richard, and her gut instinct had been that he was an honourable man.

"Yes, another good point, thank you, Natalie," said Alan, and she blushed when he praised her. She had wanted to impress him.

"Now next we have two young women. Kay was a nanny to Stephen and Chloe, and she left suddenly after Chloe died. She vanished overnight, back to her parents home in Yorkshire. Her alibi was proved to be false, as she had told us she was at home all evening on 24th May, but her friend Monique, when interviewed, told us they went to Ramsgate Harbour, then had a meal out, and came home about ten o'clock. The fact she lied is suspicious, and she ran away, so what does she have to hide? We noted that she also had designs on Stephen, and she moved in as soon as Chloe died, saying he needed her there all the time to care for Luke."

"She sounds really dodgy," announced Leanne. "The one thing in all this that is apparent is that Stephen is not only a celebrity, but also a very handsome man. Not many women would kick him out of bed."

Her words were greeted by a ripple of laughter, so having said her piece, she sat down again.

Alan had been very nervous about mentioning Monique. Initially he planned not to, but it felt dishonest, although he didn't see why the others had to know she had once been his nanny. She had only earned a low wage working for them because she was living and eating in their house, so he doubted whether she would have had the money to buy heroin. Nobody seemed that interested in her, so he could safely move on to Anna. He pointed the ruler at her photo.

"My final suspect is Anna, supposedly best friend of Chloe, but we only have her word for it. We find we can not trust her, as her opinions change from one day to the next. In the beginning, she did not like Stephen, and felt he was controlling Chloe, then after Chloe died, she seemed to think he was the greatest thing since sliced bread. During our last interview with Anna, Stephen had just given her notice to quit as Richard was moving in, so she wanted revenge, and her answers to our questions were full of accusations about them both. Her alibi was confirmed by her mother. She supposedly spent all evening with them, and went to bed at ten-thirty, but like all the other suspects, it's not beyond the realms of possibility that she could have slipped out late at night to kill Chloe, as she definitely wanted her husband."

Everybody looked at him expectantly, what was coming next? "We will be contacting Kay Wilson to find out why she lied when she gave her alibi, and I also wanted to point out that although she is not named as a suspect, Vincent Mulligan's partner Lena was very angry when she found out about his liaison with Chloe. I think in that frame of mind it's quite possible she may have gone round to the spot on the promenade and found them together."

Martha stood up, noting he had now finished speaking. "Thank you very much for that, sir, it's certainly given us all something to think about. Coffee will be served shortly, then you all have half an hour to deliberate, and then cast your vote."

"Yes, your views are very important," agreed Alan. In his mind it was still Richard that he suspected, but women had always been the more deadly of the species. Many women appeared to lust after Stephen Ward, so it could have been Anna or Kay, or alternatively Vincent's jealous girlfriend.

Alan sat down to drink his coffee. His mouth felt dry after all that speaking. The officers had separated into two groups, and were discussing theories amongst themselves. Martha sat with him, quietly contemplating. She still thought it was Stephen Ward.

When the half hour was up, they all got paper and pens, and chose the person they thought might be the culprit, and why. When Alan checked it, this was the result.

Stephen Ward had two votes, one of which was Martha; Richard Lyon had two, plus Alan's, making three; Kay Wilson had three; Anna had three and Vincent had one.

So Richard, Kay and Anna were the most voted for, with just one vote for Vincent, and none for Sam. Alan thanked them all for participating, and then headed back to his office. Of course, none of this proved anything, and what he needed to find was some hard evidence. But in the meantime, Martha had arranged a Zoom call with Kay Wilson after lunch. Alan decided if she didn't come up with a reasonable explanation, then she was going to be brought in for questioning.

Chapter Twenty-nine

Alan put on his lap top whilst in his office. Kay Wilson had become a nuisance, she had not told the truth about her alibi, and now he wanted the truth! He could see she was set up and ready to talk to him, so he clicked on the option to join the meeting. Martha, as usual was sitting with her phone set ready to record the conversation. Kay came into view, she was sitting on a sofa.

"Good afternoon, Kay. How are you today?"

"Very well, thank you."

Alan didn't intend this to last long, so he went straight to the point.

"I need you to tell me what you were doing on the evening of 24th May, and this time I want you to tell me the truth!"

Kay could tell by his tone he was annoyed, but now she was in a quandary. She had not told him about going to Ramsgate Harbour with Monique because she wanted to keep Monique out of it. She had heard nothing from her, so she didn't know what to do. Seeing her hesitation, Alan guessed why. "By the way, we know all about Monique, and how you both helped each other with false references."

Her face went pale. Was he going to arrest her for that? She didn't know, but it was obvious she needed to placate him. "I am truly sorry, I will never do that again. Yes, Monique and I helped each other, we both needed a job. On 24th May I went to Ramsgate Harbour with her, then we ate out at a little bistro close to the harbour, and we got home about ten, as it wasn't far to walk from our flats."

"Right. I wish you had told me in the first place," said Alan, grumpily.

Kay was wondering if, now he knew the truth, would herself and Monique be prosecuted. But Alan's attention was solely fixed on the murder inquiry. What they had done paled into insignificance in comparison to this.

"I should have," she said, apologetically. Alan thanked her, and told her the meeting was finished.

He went offline, and left Martha to close everything down. He hoped that was the last time he needed to speak to Kay, but he realised she had just the same opportunity as anyone else to retrace her steps back to Broadstairs that night, and kill Chloe.

James had only been going out with Jenny for three months, but he was beginning to hope they might have a future. It was her birthday today, she was twenty-eight, and he was thirty-two. He had never really had many girlfriends. Until he met Jenny, he had been married to his job, and anxious to climb the ladder of success.

James was an average looking man with a pleasant face, and Jenny liked that about him; he was kind. She was a stocky woman, and not very tall, but when she smiled her face lit up and made her look attractive. She worked in Marks and Spencer at Canterbury as a cashier in the food hall, and that was how they met. James came in to buy his lunch, and she served him.

Now, after three months only, James was beginning to realise that his job was not the be all and end all of everything. If he stayed a constable, his wages were sufficient to live on, and he would not be constantly on call as Alan was. A DCI was the most important member of the team.

He was still feeling a bit tired after their trip to Yorkshire, and then today had been the team briefing. Jenny had not been able to take a day off to celebrate her birthday because they were short staffed, so to try and make it up to her, James had booked a table at the Royal Albion Hotel, so they could enjoy a nice evening meal. She had once told him it was her favourite place.

After work had finished he nipped home to his flat in Sturry, and changed into some light slacks with a pale green shirt and tie. The Royal Albion sounded the sort of place where he should dress up, and Jenny had already said she was going to wear a new black dress that she had bought recently.

He picked her up at seven-thirty at Westbere, the little village just outside Canterbury where she lived with her parents. The Royal Albion was all that he had been expecting and more, the food was delicious, and the staff very attentive, and as he sat looking at her over the table, and she smiled at him, he was beginning to realise just how much he liked having her in his life.

James had refrained from having more than one glass of wine as he had to drive them both home later, and Jenny had also had just one, saying coyly that she didn't usually drink, but as it was her birthday, just one glass wouldn't hurt.

He had parked his car in the car park at Stone Road, as Albion Street was far too narrow to park in even at night. After paying the bill, he suggested that Jenny should stay seated until he got the car, and he would stop very briefly outside to pick her up.

As he walked down the street to the car park, he saw Richard Lyon's car coming towards him. It was unmistakable. The silver Mercedes glided into the car park, and he checked the number plate: RL 22. Oh yes, it was definitely Richard Lyon's car.

As it was now past eleven o'clock, the car park was virtually empty, except for a battered looking Ford Capri parked over at the side. James stood in the shadows and watched Richard get out of the car. He had a hooded jacket on which covered his face. This fascinated James. It wasn't the sort of thing he would expect him to wear.

Another hooded figure got out of the Capri, and they met briefly by Richard's car. Then, to his amazement, he saw the package which the other man passed to Richard. Richard took an envelope out of his hooded jacket pocket, and gave it to the man. Before James even had a chance to blink, Richard drove past him in his car, and headed back up Stone Road.

James could hardly contain himself. Richard had finally been caught out meeting his drug dealer. He knew he must contact Alan immediately! Could they finally be about to unmask the killer?

He knew it was late, but time would not matter to Alan, and he was used to being called out at odd times. James was trying to keep calm, as he also had Jenny to think about. He wanted to make sure she got safely home.

Alan's phone only rang once. He had just been drifting off to sleep, and Zoe and the children were already asleep. He grabbed it quickly from the bedside table.

"Yes James?"

"Sir, I have just seen Richard Lyon. Can't mistake his car with that number plate. He met a man in the car park by Stone Road in Broadstairs. I am sure he bought drugs, and now he is headed home."

"Oh James, this is great news. But now we have to go there and bust him. I am going to call for back-up too, in case he tries to escape. Wait for me at the beginning of Stone Road."

"I will, sir. In the meantime I must put my girlfriend in a taxi home. We have been out for a meal here tonight."

"Oh yes, make sure she it taken care of. I will get there as soon as I can."

Alan clicked his phone off, and Zoe stirred.

"Is everything OK?" she asked, sleepily.

"I have to go out, sweetheart, but yes, everything is fine."

With that he grabbed his clothes to put on. James had done so well. Had they finally found the killer?

Chapter Thirty

Richard had spent his first day over at Broadstairs with Stephen, and it was long enough for him to realise this was not going to work. His idea had been to help Stephen, and show him that caring for a baby was not that hard, but Stephen had spent most of the day shut in his office. It had been over twelve years since they had lived together, and although they had been friends for years, he didn't feel a connection any more. Stephen had become selfish and self-centred, but what worried him the most was his total lack of interest in Luke. The poor innocent little baby did not deserve this. He was already without a mother, and now had a father who did not appear to care at all. Richard vowed to himself that he would get the nanny agency to find someone as soon as they could, because right now he realised he could not trust Stephen to care of Luke whilst he was up in London at Harley Street.

During the afternoon, whilst he was feeding Luke, he had heard the study door open, and Stephen had appeared. He treated the study like it was somewhere sacred, and every time he came out of it, he locked the door. No cleaners had been allowed inside it since Stephen had claimed it. He said it was his private place where all the magic happened. Nobody argued with him, but it just seemed that, since he had lost Chloe, his stories and his fantasy world had become his crutch.

Stephen had headed out somewhere in his car without so much as a backward glance at his son and, once again, Richard had been left to feed and change him. He was almost five months old, with thick dark hair, and his blue eyes had now turned a hazel colour. As he sat on Richard's lap, he smiled at him, and he was trying hard to sit up. His heart went out to this little mite, and he couldn't help wondering what would happen to him.

Then Stephen had returned without his car, claiming it had broken down, and he had not wanted to wait for the emergency services to turn up. Something about this story did not ring true with Richard. He just knew that something was going on. He had offered to run him to the car and make sure it was parked safely, but Stephen had then told him it was at a garage the other side of Broadstairs. They had diagnosed the problem, and would be fixing it tomorrow.

Stephen seemed very withdrawn for the rest of that day. He was usually very animated when they played tennis or golf, but at home he was different. It felt almost to Richard as if Stephen had lost his way in life, and he wondered what he could do to help him.

By the time ten forty-five came round, Richard was thinking about going to bed, so he was very surprised when the study was vacated by Stephen, and he had a hooded jacket on, so was clearly going out. Stephen put on his most ingratiating smile, which had always worked with Richard.

"Can you help me out, mate. I need to go over to the other side of Broadstairs. My watch is missing, but I am pretty sure I left it in the glove compartment of my car."

Richard felt a bit irritated by this. His silver Mercedes was his pride and joy.

"Can it not wait until tomorrow?"

He was surprised to see Stephen become very stressed at that moment. It was only a watch, surely one night wouldn't hurt?

Stephen let out a sob. "It's special cos Chloe bought it for me. I need to feel it close to me, otherwise I can't cope."

Richard then felt full of guilt. Stephen had always been a sensitive man. He should have realised that he would not want to be parted from it, even for one night.

"OK mate, but please take care of it," he said, and Stephen's face broke out into a smile, and then he wiped his face with a tissue.

"I promise I won't be long," he said, and then he was gone.

At eleven-fifteen Richard heard the sound of Stephen parking his car, and relief flooded through him. He was back, and so was the car. Maybe now they could go to bed. He watched Stephen come into the kitchen. His eyes looked bright, and he seemed much more animated than when he went out.

"Did you find your watch?" he asked.

Stephen looked at him and chuckled. "You didn't believe all that baloney did you, Richard? Get ready to have a new life with me."

It hit Richard like a bolt of lightning. He couldn't believe it had taken him this long. Stephen was either drunk or on drugs. Stephen then produced a small parcel from out of his pocket, which had been opened already, and, with dread filling him, Richard knew that inside would be heroin.

"Oh, Stephen! Whatever have you done?" he said, feeling totally broken.

But Stephen was so happy, he took absolutely no notice of Richard's anguish. He lurched towards Richard, who now realised with a sinking heart, that this was the reason he locked himself in his study so much. It was not just to write.

"These little babies make me so happy. You should try them too, brother."

"I am not your brother as you well know, and heroin is not the way to get over your wife's death."

This remark made Stephen roar with laughter. "Who says I want to get over her death? All I want is you and I to be happy. We make a great couple, ya know."

Richard went pale. All of a sudden the pieces of a jigsaw were coming together to make the picture, but it was a picture that he did not want to see. "So it was you that killed her then. . ." he said, huskily.

Stephen puffed out his chest. He was feeling so good, everything was going so well in his life.

"Well, ya know she had it coming. Wearing that scarf round her neck made it so easy. I already knew the kid wasn't mine, but it wasn't until you arrived that night, and I was able to go up to the funfair, that I found her talking to that gypsy. He didn't want to know about the kid, but I could have told him Luke was his."

Richard was shocked. Even though he had been Chloe's doctor and confidante, she had never mentioned any of this. "But you can't know that for sure."

Stephen gave a raucous laugh. He was obviously very high. His eyes looked wild, which sickened Richard. This was not the Stephen he had once loved. This man absolutely sickened him.

"But I do know. Five years ago I had an infection in my testes, so bad that one of them had to be removed. I tested sterile after that. I even need hormone pills to keep me male."

"Why didn't you tell me. I might have been able to help you."

Stephen laughed again. It was a weird laugh; not friendly, almost mocking.

"You were too busy with Ed."

He had touched a nerve by mentioning Ed, and his mocking attitude was not helping.

"Don't speak about him like that," Richard said, still trying to digest the fact that his best friend Stephen had killed his own wife. It just seemed unreal.

Now Stephen became very vocal, and shouting loudly at the top of his voice, he said, "Richard, you know we can be good together. You love me. I killed her so we could live in this great house together, or even sell it and go back to London."

"Stop your dreaming, Stephen. There is no us. Now I understand why she was all over the place, and the mood swings, you were giving her heroin," he said, with horror sweeping through him at the thought of it.

"Yes, I tried to wear her down," boasted Stephen, "but she was a tough cookie to break. I hid empty bottles everywhere so the nanny would think she had been drinking. Then there were the mood swings, as well."

"Why are you telling me all this? You know the police will catch up with you!" said Richard, desperately. Regardless of their past, he could not allow Stephen to get away with this.

"Honesty, of course. I killed her for you, Richard, so we could have a life together. Even a child. You are so good with Luke!"

Richard had never been a violent man, and he had a calm disposition usually, but right now he felt he would not be responsible for his actions towards Stephen.

"Don't you dare blame me for your evil actions!" he roared. Something took hold of him, and he felt he wanted to choke the very life out of this murderer. He lunged towards him, and at that selfsame moment there was a loud rap at the front door, and voices boomed out.

"Police here! Let us in! We are armed!"

Stephen glanced wildly around him, then tossed his packet in the direction of Richard. With a quick movement he sped across the hall and up the stairs. Richard heard the study door close, and Stephen was gone.

Richard was shaking with fear now, as he went out into the hall and opened the front door. Armed police pushed their way into the house, followed by Alan. As his eyes met Richard's and spotted the offending parcel of drugs, he acted swiftly. Assisted by James, who put the handcuffs on Richard, Alan moved down the hallway. "Richard Lyon, I am arresting you for the murder of Chloe Ward. You do not need to say anything, but if you do so, it will be taken down, and may be used in evidence."

"No, oh no, you've got it all wrong," sobbed Richard, totally devastated.

"Yes, that's what they all say!" said James, grimly. "I guess that packet contains heroin."

Alan placed the open packet into a plastic bag. At last they had evidence.

Richard was desperate. He could see his whole life as a doctor vanishing before his eyes, and a life in prison beckoning. "Truly, it's not me, it's Stephen. He's a very mentally sick man. He has locked himself in his study, and he's high on drugs now."

James and Alan exchanged glances. "But you went to get them. I saw you in your car," James said.

"No, it wasn't me, Stephen borrowed my car," said Richard.

Alan thought quickly. This might be true, they might have arrested the wrong man. Richard looked like a broken man, not a criminal. He turned towards the armed officers.

"Right, let's get him out of the study."

There was a stampede for the stairs. James was behind with Richard, who was still handcuffed.

"Open the door, we are armed!" was the cry, but there was no response. After a nod to one another they crashed the door in, and such a sight met their eyes. Even with the windows open, the unmistakable stench of drugs assaulted their senses. But on the desk, right next to Stephen's lap top were scraps of tissues, carelessly abandoned when the contents had been used. There was rubbish everywhere. Unlike the rest of the house, this room was filthy.

The windows in the room were old fashioned French windows, which led out to a tiny ledge overlooking the garden. They were three floors up, and dangling on the edge of the ledge was Stephen, who laughed maniacally when he saw the police.

"So the troops are here. Good evening, gentlemen. Yes, it was me. I killed Chloe, and gave her heroin, but she didn't know about it. I mixed it in her food."

Alan felt sickened by his words. His anger was so strong, he felt that if Stephen jumped, he would do them all a favour. James seemed to be rooted to the spot. But suddenly Alan thought about why he was in the force. He wanted to keep the public safe, and even the most evil of criminals deserved to live and maybe have a chance to reform. It was not up to him to judge. He walked slowly into the room and towards the window ledge, whilst talking in a low voice to Stephen.

"Stephen, if you fall down there, you won't be a pretty sight. Now, you don't want to die. Think of all those stories you have written with happy endings."

He was almost within touching distance now, and with the mention of stories, Stephen's face took on a rapturous expression. In his state of euphoria he had visions of himself writing meaningful love stories in a prison cell.

"Can I have my own cell?" His euphoria was starting to wear off now, and when he looked down he felt dizzy. The concrete below did not look inviting.

Alan took one more step, and then quickly grabbed at Stephen's leg, which made Stephen overbalance. He yelled with fear, but Alan hung on grimly, he wasn't going to give up on him now.

Within minutes the armed police had helped to get Stephen down, and he was handcuffed. Richard was also still in handcuffs, so Alan decided to leave them on for now, and then take them both to the police station. He read Stephen his rights, and then they were both escorted out to a police car.

The noise had attracted interest, and although it was very late, there was a small group of neighbours gathered within viewing distance of the police car.

As the police car pulled away, Alan turned towards the small crowd of neighbours.

"Sorry to disturb you all. Everything is OK now, you can all sleep safely."

They all moved away, and James was standing there beside him.

"I was wrong about Richard. Poor Richard. It was obvious how guilty Stephen was," he said, thoughtfully. "But it's all thanks to you, James. I will definitely mention you for promotion."

James beamed with delight. "Glad to be of help, sir, but you saved his life. If he had jumped off that ledge! Did you think he was worth saving?"

"A good question," said Alan, "but I cannot play God. We have to protect the public from people like him. One day, if he reforms, he may be a useful member of society, but I am not holding my breath."

A policeman came out of the house carrying Luke, who was wide awake and crying lustily.

"I am taking this little chap back as well," he said, sadly.

"Give him here a minute," said Alan, and the man handed him over. Alan cuddled him gently, talking softly to him. Luke gazed at him with interest, and stopped crying. "There you go," said Alan, handing him back.

"What will happen to him? It's very sad," said James.

Alan sighed. It was true, a poor little orphan, yet there were people like Monique who would welcome him with open arms. He thought of his own family, and they felt even more precious.

"It is sad, but he will go to foster parents, and they will give him stability," he said, firmly. He always tried not to take his job home with him.

"Come on now, James. We have homes to go to, and tomorrow is another day."